Mirror
Blue

Mirror Blue

Thomma Lyn Grindstaff

Black Lyon Publishing, LLC

MIRROR BLUE
Copyright © 2009 by THOMMA GRINDSTAFF

Our books may be ordered through your local bookstore or by visiting the publisher:

www.BlackLyonPublishing.com

Black Lyon Publishing, LLC
PO Box 567
Baker City, OR 97814

This is a work of fiction. All of the characters, names, events, organizations and conversations in this novel are either the products of the author's vivid imagination or are used in a fictitious way for the purposes of this story.

ISBN-10:   1-934912-16-4
ISBN-13:   978-1-934912-16-6
Library of Congress Control Number: 2009924904

Written, published and printed in
the United States of America.

Black Lyon Literary Love Story

To my beloved husband, without whose love this book would not have been written. You are my muse, and you are the song I will sing forever.

Sometimes a troop of damsels glad,
An abbot on an ambling pad,
Sometimes a curly shepherd-lad,
Or long-hair'd page in crimson clad,
Goes by to tower'd Camelot;
And sometimes thro' the mirror blue
The knights come riding two and two:
She hath no loyal knight and true,
The Lady of Shalott.

But in her web she still delights
To weave the mirror's magic sights,
For often thro' the silent nights
A funeral, with plumes and lights
And music, went to Camelot:
Or when the moon was overhead,
Came two young lovers lately wed:
"I am half sick of shadows," said
The Lady of Shalott.

From "The Lady of Shalott"
Alfred, Lord Tennyson

1. Groupie

Aphra reached up and sighed in relief when she touched her hair instead of her motorcycle helmet. Thank goodness she hadn't worn the helmet inside the bookstore. When she went places on Wilbur, her Harley-Davidson motorcycle, she often forgot to take off her helmet. She wanted to hurry to the bathroom and brush her hair, but only one person was ahead of her in line, a backpack-toting young man, and a bunch of people had come in behind her. She didn't want to lose her place. If she did, she might lose her nerve.

She felt like a groupie. Why had she come?

Perhaps she'd come out of desperation, searching for a spark to blast herself out of irrelevancy, seeking to prevent those around her from making her feel useless.

Isaac Lightfoot: Aphra's favorite author since she was fourteen and had read his first novel for a class assignment. He was a Vietnam veteran who wrote as though he commanded a line of sight to whatever ideal forms cast mere shadows in other authors' literary caves. Wounded in combat, recipient of numerous medals and citations, he was also something of an East Tennessee celebrity. One of Knoxville's own. Or close to it. Isaac Lightfoot was from the adjoining community of Solway.

Only a few people knew of Aphra's admiration for him: her family and Isaac Lightfoot himself, if he remembered a reverential letter he'd received almost two decades ago from a lonely teenage girl. She'd kept the reply she received from him: a note giving every indication of having been composed with care, appreciative of her effusive sentiments, telling her he looked forward to reading, someday, a novel she'd written.

But he probably said that to all the girls.

The backpack-toting young man moved away, and it was Aphra's turn. Isaac Lightfoot regarded her from his desk, lips curved in a slight smile, blue eyes genial behind silver-rimmed spectacles with tear drop shaped lenses. He looked spry, but after a long book tour, he was probably glad to be home.

From the photos on the back of his books, Aphra recognized his lush mustache and close-clipped, gray and brown beard; from the interviews he'd given on the public broadcasting channel, she was familiar with his rumbly voice; yet she feared that if taken in large enough doses, the man in three dimensions would bowl her aside with his physicality. It was hard for her to believe they were sharing the same space.

She couldn't maintain eye contact, so she stared at his big shoulder. Strange to be face-to-face with a person who had figured so highly and for so long in her private realm. She felt rude, shoving him out of it and making him real.

"Hi there," he said, helping her.

Say her piece or die of shame. She shifted her gaze from his shoulder back to his eyes, rain-saturated stratus clouds with cores of molten lead. She found their slight asymmetry disconcertingly sensual.

"Hi, Mr. Lightfoot. I guess I've been reading your books for, oh, twenty years now." She hoped he'd forgive her banality.

"Please call me Isaac." He pointed at the novel she held. "Which book have you got there?"

"*The Smallest Survivor.*" His newest novel, it was the story of a young boy's fight to survive in the frigid ruins of Stalingrad during the height of the World War II battle. Should Aphra tell him that not once while reading the last hundred pages did she stop crying, tears of rage, tears of sorrow, tears of laughter, sometimes all three at the same time? She could discuss the novel with him for hours. Days. But they had only minutes.

"You made little Oleg so real that sometimes, reading the book, I thought I saw him out of the corner of my eye," Aphra said.

"He's based on my son, Sam. At least on how Sam was when he was little. He's not so little now."

Aphra recalled the author bios on the back of his books. Most of them said "Isaac Lightfoot lives in Knoxville, Tennessee with his wife, Norma. They have a son, Sam." Norma. What a lucky woman Norma was, to be Isaac Lightfoot's wife. But the author bios for his two most recent novels hadn't mentioned Norma. He wore no wedding ring, but from the pictures Aphra had seen of him over the years, he never had. Perhaps he'd decided to keep his private life more private.

"Well, you did a great job with the novel." Aphra wished she could think of something more to say.

It wasn't only his writing style that captivated her, though words in sumptuous juxtaposition moved her as surely as the strains of a grand orchestral suite.

The strongest pull was made of this: whether as a lonely, teenage nerd, a restless college student, or a thirty-three year-old woman on the cusp of stagnancy or liberation, she perceived the essence of his words and knew he somehow understood her; she felt that if she were a man or he were a woman, they would be, in either case, close to the same person.

Oh my. She was being ridiculous.

"Thanks, Mrs.? Miss?"

"Miss. My name's Aphra Porter."

"That's an unusual name." He paused. "Wait a minute. Aphra wouldn't be a nickname for Aphrodite, would it?"

"It would." Aphra considered herself lucky. Her mom had almost named her Persephone, and her nickname would have been Percy. It was a horror beyond imagining.

Isaac scrutinized her. "I recollect a letter I got, oh, a long time ago, from a young girl who signed it Aphrodite Porter. Was that you?"

After eighteen years, he remembered her letter! Aphra nodded, suffused by joy, and her words pushed themselves out between its cracks. "That's me. I wrote you a letter when I was fifteen." She blushed, remembering why she'd signed it "Aphrodite" for its evocations of love and beauty, emphasis on love even if she hadn't felt beautiful. What a goose she'd been.

"I was pretty near blown away by a teenage girl enjoying my books, and I was impressed with your writing skills," he said. "And your name is pretty."

Aphra was relaxing into this. "I'm Aphrodite Rhea, and my sister is Diana Ceres. When Di and I were born, my parents were hippies from heck. Daddy's a philosophy professor, so you know he's way out there, and Mom's into mythology and fantasy lit. I guess Di and I should consider ourselves lucky we didn't wind up named after trolls, dwarves, or ancient philosophers."

"What're your folks' names then? Cronus and Gaea?"

"Nothing so exotic. Plain old Larry and Barb."

Isaac grinned broadly, and neither he nor Aphra looked away. Feet shuffled behind her, and Aphra realized she was taking up too much of Isaac's time. There had to be twenty-five people behind her now.

"Do you still write?" he asked, in no hurry to move her along. "In your letter, you said you liked to write stories."

"I've written short stories, yes, but I don't submit them anywhere. I'm afraid of rejection. Maybe I'm afraid I don't have much to say. Anyway, I do freelance Web site design, mainly for folks here in town. I can't deal with the nine-to-five workaday thing." You're babbling, she told herself and stopped.

"Something tells me you've got plenty to say. And Web site design sounds interesting. I bet you could give my site a face lift." Isaac winked at her and, reduced to primordial ooze, she managed to pass him her copy of *The Smallest Survivor.* Surely he was kidding about the Web site. Bantering. Well, he could banter with her all he liked. She didn't mind.

As he took the novel, their fingers brushed. Aphra probably imagined that he prolonged his part of the touch. Why would he? "Does your son write?" She was genuinely curious.

"No, he's a mechanic. He's got his own little shop right outside town. He's married, and just the other week, he told me his wife's expecting. One day come autumn, I'm going to wake up a grandpa."

"Yeah, me too," Aphra replied. "Sometime in November." Why was Isaac chuckling?

"That's some trick," he said. "You'll be the youngest, prettiest grandpa around."

"Oh my. I meant, I recently found out I'm going to be an Aunt." She laughed, too. How could he think she was pretty, covered in cat hair, wearing a mountain man jacket? Pretty isn't pretty compared to a gaggle of grandfathers.

"Must be something in the water." Isaac turned his attention to the book Aphra had handed him and stroked his mustache before beginning to write. The sound of grumbling behind Aphra rose to compete with the noise of shuffling feet.

Watching him write on the inside front cover of the book, Aphra was amazed by how long she'd been his fan. From online biographies she'd read, Aphra knew that he was fifty-three. His first novel, *Red Sands*—the one she'd read in eighth grade—had been published when he was thirty-one, and his first non-fiction book, about the origins of the Vietnam debacle, must have been written when he was in his mid-twenties.

Life was passing Aphra by, and all she was doing was sitting and staring at its coattails until they disappeared around the corner. Was her sigh audible? It must have been, because Isaac looked up. Perish any thought in his head that she was impatient! No, he'd finished writing in her book and wanted to hand it back. She wished she could wait until she got home to savor what he'd written, but she couldn't keep herself from opening the book.

"To Aphra," asserted the confident, precise hand she recognized from his long-ago letter. "A light burning, a beacon in the dark. You can do it. Isaac Lightfoot."

She sucked in a deep breath to equalize pressure with the happy noise that wanted to escape, holding it in to maintain the tatters of her dignity. And she thought she'd felt like a groupie waiting in line!

"Thank you," Aphra said. "You're a—" She had to start again. "You're my inspiration." That's enough, shut up. How lovely it would be to shake his hand, but she couldn't bear to offer hers. Emotional as she was at that moment, they must part cleanly. At any rate, his right hand was occupied—he was scribbling in vain on a notepad. His ball point pen had run out of ink.

"Well, I appreciate you, too. It's people like you who make me feel like I'm doing something worthwhile." He retrieved another pen from his desk and smiled at her. It was a smile he wore all over his face but particularly in his eyes.

As she left the bookstore, the afternoon sunlight struck her as obnoxious. She could happily reside in the store as long as Isaac Lightfoot were there, too. But sooner or later he'd go home to his family, and there Aphra would be, alone on the sterile tile. His life wasn't about his fans.

She tucked *The Smallest Survivor* into the carry-all buckled around her waist, leaving her earbuds, snug against her portable

CD player, untouched.

The grandeur of the Baroque and the rhythms of psychedelic rock were both perfect fits with the open road. Her custom was to blare Handel, Bach, Hendrix, or Led Zeppelin into her ears as she rode, depending on her mood.

But not today.

She peeked over her shoulder for one last glimpse of Isaac in the flesh, if also through the glass. His pen was poised over someone else's book, but he was looking in her direction.

Was he watching her? She couldn't be sure. Her image was superimposed over his.

Reaching her motorcycle, Aphra noticed a dark red, early-eighties model Jeep Scrambler with a tan soft top and a Tennessee plate on the back that said "Vietnam Veteran"—Isaac's vehicle, no doubt, parked at the head of the next row over. The Scrambler was like him in the same way that Wilbur was like Aphra. Some people matched their mode of transportation the way other people resembled their pets.

Her adventure had gone better than she'd dared hope. She and Isaac Lightfoot had been, for a brief time, a Mutual Appreciation Society of Two. That was kind of a connection, wasn't it?

As she rode away, Aphra didn't know why she was crying, though her tears were constrained to her helmet and she had no trouble seeing the road ahead.

2. Unique Search String

"Meow!"

Aphra was being summoned.

Lounging in her La-Z Girl, rereading *The Smallest Survivor*, she shifted her feet to the edge of the footrest to allow maximum space for Pilar, newly arrived on the chair. Pilar throttled up a smooth purr and rested her head between Aphra's sock-clad feet. Aphra didn't know what it was about her lower extremities that entranced Pilar so. Nor could Aphra fathom Pilar's enmity toward coffee stirrers—the thin sipping straws she plucked out of coffee mugs then batted onto the floor.

As Aphra admired Pilar's fluffy resplendence, someone else jumped from the end table near her elbow to the back of her La-Z Girl and began kneading her head with vigorous paws. Her impromptu masseuse was Santiago, her James Dean in a Cat Suit, her Rebel Without Claws—his previous owners had declawed him in a former life unknown to Aphra.

Pilar was a rescue from the pound, Santiago a rescue from the street. Each was spoiled and adored. The condo Aphra rented was a Cathouse. Coffee stirrers lay scattered like Pick-up Stix, perches for scenic catnapping were installed at the windows, and scratching posts rose like obelisks from catnip-seasoned carpet.

She returned to *The Smallest Survivor*, but not before glancing fondly at the inscription left by Isaac Lightfoot a week ago. She'd allotted herself an hour to read before returning to work on a Web site she was designing for a local realtor. Hopefully, she'd finish the site tonight.

But her Isaac Lightfoot Interlude wasn't to last. The doorbell rang.

"Damn." Aphra thumped *The Smallest Survivor* down on the

end table. Why couldn't people call before they came over? She dislodged Santiago from her head and Pilar from her feet and rose from the La-Z Girl to admit her uninvited guest.

Through the peephole, she spied Tony Farthing standing on her doorstep, his expression embodying all the dopey earnestness of a blue-tick hound. She opened the door and endeavored to lower her surliness quotient, though she didn't go overboard feigning a happy face.

"Hey, Alf." Tony stepped inside and looked around. Aphra fancied he'd been panting. "Nice place you've got here. Look, I hope I'm not bothering you, but I just came from Trev and Di's, and Di told me you had a copy of *Shimmering Seascape* I could borrow. I guess I'm the only person in the country who hasn't seen it."

Yes, Di lived five minutes away, but Aphra's residence wasn't an extension of hers. How, Aphra thought, did one go about lobotomizing one's sister? Di knew she liked to work at night. And why must Tony call her Alf, her family's nickname for her? It sounded weird, coming from him. She wished he'd call her Aphra.

Because Tony had been best friends with Trevor, Di's husband, since childhood, Di couldn't shake the delusion that Tony and Aphra would fall in love and do the Happily Ever After Thing; then Trevor and Tony and Di and Aphra would be a blissful foursome, sending their children to school together and ushering them to the Fields of Nirvana for dual-family outings of cavorting and catching butterflies.

Leading Tony through the living room, which was now bereft of cats, Aphra pulled a DVD from her entertainment rack and handed it to him. He sat on the loveseat and she returned to her La-Z Girl. She didn't recline, but she did try to chill out. Tony was nice, if dense. And it wasn't his fault if Di told him it was okay to drop by.

"As far as I'm concerned, you can keep the movie. Di gave it to me for my birthday. She loves it, but honestly, I don't like it much. It's too cutesy for me." Aphra held back the harshest part of her criticism. Tony might like it. To Aphra's mind, however, if she butchered every sacred cow in the film, she'd be eating hamburger every day for the next twenty years. If she accidentally ingested poison, *Shimmering Seascape* would be an effective stand-in for ipecac. A recent Hollywood blockbuster about the World War

II era that paralleled the trials of American soldiers abroad with the tribulations of women on the home front, the movie broke no new ground and was instead downright reactionary: it depicted marriage as nothing more than a holding pen for children and women as brood hens who were more concerned about having their men's babies than they were about their men. Where the hell was Rosie the Riveter in that movie?

Isaac Lightfoot would loathe *Shimmering Seascape*.

How odd to think about Isaac Lightfoot while looking at Tony. Aphra superimposed her memory of Isaac, brawny and straight-shouldered at his desk in the bookstore, over the reality of Tony, slight and boneless on her loveseat.

"I'm surprised you don't like it," Tony said. "Even women who hate war movies like *Shimmering Seascape*. I think you're the only woman I've talked to who doesn't like it."

"I'm also the only woman you know who rides a hog," Aphra pointed out.

"True. Anyhow, I'll check out the movie. The previews looked pretty good."

"Yeah, I enjoyed the previews. They were action-oriented, though, and the combat scenes in the movie are fine. It's the home front scenes that bugged me. They're smarmy as all get-out. Surely society's saccharine content wasn't that much higher sixty years ago than it is today."

"Well, I think that's the point of the movie. It's supposed to have a positive message, taking us back to when things were simpler, when people knew what was up. Back, you know, to those more innocent times…"

Poor Tony, Aphra thought. He should stick to recaps of baseball games. In games, what you saw was what you got. And innocent times? Isaac Lightfoot's father, Samuel, who stormed the beaches at Normandy, might disagree, were he still around to say his piece. And what of the women who worked themselves ragged for the war effort and who struggled, despite significant privation, to care for themselves so they could, in turn, care for others who needed them, known and unknown, young and old, home and abroad? The women in *Shimmering Seascape* were all about "I want, I want" and were reduced to wailing wretches when they didn't "get." Invertebrates, all. What about the real women who sacrificed, women who lost, who hurt, but who had sufficient backbone to keep from whining and keep on trucking?

While Tony rambled on about the movie, the white-whiskered, orange visage of Pilar peeked into the living room from the hall, intent on reconnoitering her perimeter. Though Santiago played at being a bad ass, it was Pilar who was Aphra's Commando Cat: she kept her tail high and her claws sharp.

"Are you allergic to cats?" Aphra asked, interrupting Tony, who stopped speaking as though his plug had been pulled.

"Just a little bit. But you know what, it goes away the more I'm around them."

Oh my, Aphra thought. If that wasn't a hint, she didn't know what was.

"I think it's neat that Trev and Di are going to have a baby," Tony said. "It's about time, huh? I can't wait to be a kinda-sorta Uncle. I'm crazy about kids."

"Well, I prefer cats," Aphra said. "And between you and me, I don't know that it's such a great idea for them to have a kid, with all their bills and Di being so busy at the store. But I'm sure they'll do the best they can." She couldn't resist prodding askew those rose-hued glasses of his. Reality was an unpleasant thing for many people to contemplate. Sometimes for her, too.

"You've got a point," Tony said, to Aphra's surprise. "That's sure a big monthly payment they got stuck with. And it's not even a very big house. Makes me appreciate my apartment – at least the rent is cheap. Anyway, I'll get to be around lots of kids come May. I'm going to start coaching a tee ball team."

It wasn't something Aphra would want to do. School playgrounds and baseball diamonds harbored bothersome associations for a woman like her who'd been a solitary and ridiculed child, but more power to him. "I hope you have fun with it."

Pilar entered the room and tiptoed toward Tony. Cautiously, she approached his shoe.

"Here, kitty, kitty." He reached down to pet her, but she shimmied away, did an abrupt right-face, and exited the living room, her tail held high in the air like a fluffy torch.

Emulating her cat, Aphra took the direct approach. "Tony, I'm sorry. I don't want to be rude, but I'm buried up to my eyeballs in Web site stuff." It wasn't exactly true. After finishing the realtor's site, Aphra expected a comparative lull during which she hoped to start writing a novel. Or at least a new short story. But Tony didn't have to know that. "Would you mind if we called it a night?"

Tony looked startled, but was he startled by Aphra's words or by her cat? Accustomed to Di's mollycoddling, he might expect the same from her sister. Yet according to Di, Tony liked Aphra because she was "full of surprises."

Sigh.

"No problem." Tony peeled himself from Aphra's loveseat. "I didn't think you'd be busy on a Saturday. Di should have told me." Yes, Di should have told him. "It's okay," Aphra said.

Hovering at his elbow, she encouraged Tony doorward, making sure he had *Shimmering Seascape* well in hand so he wouldn't have to return for it. He cast her a beseeching look.

"Will you double me on your bike sometime? I haven't been on motorcycles much, but Di says you can really handle that Harley, and I'd love to see how it rides."

Why did he keep trying to wrangle some semblance of a date from her? "Sorry, Tony, I don't double people." Her words came out too fast. Aphra hoped he didn't know that she occasionally doubled Di when Di made her promise to go slow. If he did know, she hoped he wasn't boorish enough to point it out.

He said only, "Well then, I'll see you soon." Not "see you later" but "see you soon." As though he expected to. Presumed to. The assumption riled Aphra. She didn't have anything against Tony. She just didn't have anything for him, either.

She responded with, "See you later."

When she turned back to the living room, she saw both her cats sitting there as though they'd never left.

There would be no more re-reading tonight. *The Smallest Survivor* must remain, postponed but not forgotten, on her end table. It was time to spurn her La-Z Girl for her office chair.

In her office, she spun a web as surely as any spider, but her job was to make it pleasing to the fly. To do so, she edited frames, tweaked colors, resized digital photos, modified image maps, and added links. She'd already completed much of the legwork over the past week; what remained to be done tonight was to pull everything together into a coherent package.

And after five hours of effort, Aphra could say she'd done so.

She took pride in her work—building Web sites from the ground up and redesigning existing ones – and she was sure Joyce-Ann McGaha and her cohorts at McGaha Realty would appreciate the care she'd taken with their company's Digital Face to the World.

While Pilar and Santiago twined around her ankles, serenading her with purrs and cat chat, Aphra verified the functionality of the site. Then she opened her e-mail program to write a note to Joyce-Ann letting her know that the site was ready for testing. Aphra didn't expect a reply from her until tomorrow; after all, it was two o'clock in the morning, a peak hour for Aphra and her cats but not for most people.

Her program checked for new mail on startup, and tonight she had the usual twenty or so messages. She composed a message to Joyce-Ann and sent it, then she examined the Sender fields of the messages in her Inbox. There were two forwarded jokes from Di, five messages from clients, no doubt with tech support questions about work Aphra had done for them in the past, five newsletters packed with resources for freelance Web site designers, and three chunks of Spam that suffered the swift judgment of her delete key. She scrolled down to see the remaining messages, but further inventory was made impossible when she spied the Sender field of the second message from the bottom, which read: Isaac W. Lightfoot. Subject: You've got a mighty fine Web site. It was time-stamped one in the morning. An hour ago.

In what universe had Aphra stumbled? And how, pray tell, could she stay there?

He'd been serious at the book signing with his comment about his Web site. No bantering, just fact.

Her fingers were ice cold on her trackball. Maybe a pernicious address-gathering virus was responsible for the e-mail and Isaac Lightfoot hadn't written her at all.

But he had. The message read: "Dear Aphrodite: I'm writing you via the e-mail link you provided on your Web site, which I found through the Allegro search engine, describing your Web site design services. You must be aware that your name constitutes a unique search string (here, he had inserted a smiley emoticon).

"My official author's Web site with Pace & Rafferty Publishing is in desperate need of a fresh look. Indeed, its design, or lack thereof, could be touted by pharmaceutical companies as a miracle cure for insomnia. Happily, P & R's not-so-technically-oriented division is critically understaffed these days, and they've agreed to my enlisting a competent freelance designer to pull me out of my electronic tar pit of stodginess. Perusal of your Web site tells me that you would be an excellent choice.

"If you are available to lend a hand, please contact me either by e-mail or by telephone. Sincerely and warm regards, Isaac Lightfoot.

"P.S.—How could I go wrong with a Web site designer who rides a purple Harley? I saw you take off after you left the bookstore. You have excellent taste."

His telephone number —home?—followed his signature.

Warm regards, yes. If he knew how warm she was feeling right now.

Isaac Lightfoot's site was painfully dull. Aphra would know: she'd had it bookmarked for the six years since it was created, and it hadn't been updated in three of those years.

She, Aphra, spending time with Isaac Lightfoot.

They might become friends. Dare she think the M word; that was, Mentor?

She replied with a note giving enthusiastic assent, then she leaned back in her chair to savor her good fortune.

Following completion of a Web project, she usually took Wilbur for an o'dark thirty ride, unwinding to the growl of his engine on roads free of traffic, music, routed into her mind from her earbuds, buffeting her like high wind.

But the Midnight Rider could do nothing now but sit.

And sit.

And grin.

Santiago batted her ankle. What's up with you, Mom? he seemed to ask.

Life rolled along for lengthy stretches, straight as unyielding concrete, but oh, those occasional, twisty trails!

3. Autumn's Breath Burning

Two minutes before noon, when Isaac Lightfoot was due to knock on Aphra's door, Pilar left a large deposit in her litterbox. When you had to go, you had to go, and Aphra was glad her cats were healthy; nonetheless, Pilar's timing was less than optimal. Aphra performed the Scooping Ritual to ensure that Isaac's first impression of her home wouldn't be defined by Parfum de Cat Poop.

When she heard the anticipated knock, however, she realized that her triumph was short-lived, for Santiago now squatted in his plastic throne. At least he covered what he left.

Isaac was right on time. Perhaps it was true that soldiers' watches became extensions of their wrists.

Since the book signing two weeks ago, Isaac had dwelled in Aphra's thoughts exactly as he had appeared that day. And when she opened the door, it was as though he'd sprung, fully-formed, from her mind. Each feature was intact: his imposing build, his short, brown hair sprinkled with gray, the blue eyes, the bearded, chiseled jaw. And there were the silver-rimmed spectacles and the snake skin cowboy boots.

Wait. She didn't remember snake skin cowboy boots from the book signing. She hadn't seen his feet that day. And he was holding a three-ring binder out of which peeped a manila envelope – no doubt the text and photographs he was bringing for his Web site. He smelled of light, woodsy cologne. This, then, was the real Isaac Lightfoot, not the denizen of her dreams.

She still couldn't grasp that she was lucky enough for this to be happening.

Professional, freelance Web site designers didn't gawp open-mouthed at their clients. Aphra recovered herself and invited him inside, then gestured toward the hall. "Come on into my office, Mr.

Light—I mean, Isaac. It's the room with the least amount of cat hair."

In truth, though, there wasn't much cat hair in the living room, nor was the carpet sprinkled with catnip and coffee stirrers. Aphra ran the vacuum cleaner—"The Monster" to her cats—yesterday. Of the cats themselves, not a whisker could be seen. Santiago must have given a hasty response to nature's call.

"I like cats just fine, so their hair shouldn't be a problem," Isaac said.

Isaac followed Aphra to her office, and she indicated a chair at the table she kept there for clients. She moved her other chair to a respectful distance, then sat down. Being too close to Isaac made Aphra jittery. Why? she wondered. She wasn't afraid of him. Actually, she felt safe with him: she was, after all, in the company of a former Army Ranger and decorated combat veteran – an uncommonly courageous man.

Maybe it was her reaction to him that frightened her. She was a comet plunging perilously close to the searing sun—her icy shell was melting to form a tail that would follow ten-million miles in her wake.

But if she maintained trajectory, keeping the tail well behind her, perhaps he wouldn't notice it.

Isaac's expression was impassive as he leafed through his notebook. Aphra was glad one of them had some sense.

A moment passed, then he placed the notebook on the table. He flipped to the first page and took out a compact disc and a few pictures from the manila envelope. "I typed everything for you because I don't want you to wear your fingers out. All this text is saved on CD. And I brought some pictures that ought to look nice. Well, since they're pictures of me, 'nice' is a relative term. At least the camera didn't break."

"It's hard to believe you've destroyed any cameras." How could Isaac not know how handsome he was?

Aphra reined in her thoughts to the matter at hand: Web site design. She and Isaac had discussed money on the telephone, and he wanted to pay her well. In truth, though, she'd build his site for free. Why concern herself with money when she'd been blessed by Fortune: it was rare that an aspiring novelist got the chance to do a favor for her muse.

Over the next half-hour, they worked their way through the notebook, and Aphra scribbled notes in the margins. Isaac had left much to her judgment, and she was honored by his trust. He referred to his son in the text he had prepared, but he didn't mention his wife. Had they divorced? Were they separated? Did they have one hell of a fight? Aphra would love to know, but she wouldn't dream of asking. It was none of her business.

After they had reviewed the last page of the notebook, Isaac said, "Well, I thank you for your help on my site. I know you'll turn it into something special." He was awkward, different from his plucky incarnation at the book signing. Did she make him uncomfortable? The idea was painful. Aphra had always been shy, and she had yet to find a middle ground between reserve and overcompensation, neither of which tended to put people at ease.

"I'll do my best." She cast out mental hooks, hoping to snag a savory conversational fish to keep him at her table, but today's business was done. She'd never become friends with clients. Why should things be different with him? To think she'd entertained notions of having him read her short stories. Could she be a bigger fool?

Isaac made no move to leave, however. Instead, he glanced toward the doorway that led into the hall. Following his gaze, Aphra saw Pilar the Commando Cat entering the office, her whiskers bristling. Isaac stretched out his hand, keeping it at kitty nose level, a foot or so above the carpet. He winked at Aphra but otherwise remained still. Oh, Isaac's winks!

At the offering of Isaac's hand, Pilar stopped and squatted on her haunches. When Isaac made no further overtures, Pilar slowly moved forward again and kept coming until her nose was a hair's breadth from his hand. She sniffed, covering his fingers and his broad palm in turn. Evidently, Pilar liked what she smelled, because she rubbed against Isaac's hand with one furry cheek then the other, purring like a chainsaw run amok, as though he were made of catnip.

It was the first time Aphra had ever been envious of her cat.

When Isaac leaned back, the Commando Cat morphed into his Handy Dandy Boot Polisher.

"Looks like you made a friend," Aphra said. She couldn't stop grinning even if she wanted to.

"I reckon so." Isaac watched Pilar as she draped herself lovingly around his boots. "That's one good looking cat you've got there. What's his name?"

"I know she's big, but she's a girl kitty. Her name is Pilar. Consider yourself honored, because she seldom takes to people so quickly."

"Is she your only cat?"

"Nope, I have one more—Santiago. Before long, he'll be meandering in here, now that Pilar has surveyed the area and found only friendlies."

Before Isaac could respond, the phone rang. Aphra picked up the extension on her desk. It didn't occur to her that she could have excused herself and taken the call in the living room until after she'd answered it.

It was Di. "Hi, Alf. Tony is here visiting, and he wants me to ask you if it's a good time for him to run that movie back by your place."

"No. Not a good time. I have a client here."

"Oh, my God! How could I have forgotten? And how can you say it like that, a client, like it's just any old boring person, a realtor, an insurance agent or someone? It's Isaac Lightfoot, your heartthrob, who's over there, isn't it?"

Aphra visualized the mock leer that must be spreading across Di's puckish face. Sisters. You'd think by now a cure would have been found. Why did Aphra tell her anything? "Yeah, yeah. Just tell Tony he'll have to run the movie by later, okay?"

Di giggled. "Try not to slip on the puddle of drool you're leaving on the floor. I'd hate for you to break your neck."

Isaac couldn't possibly miss the blush that scorched her face. She could kick herself for not taking Di's call in her office. "You're a cold woman, Diana Ceres. I'll talk to you later."

As she reclaimed her spot beside Isaac, she saw Santiago sitting in the hall, absorbing the office tableau. Isaac, however, was oblivious to the newly-arrived kitty. His expression was remote, as though carved of granite, and his eyes seemed to see nothing. Aphra thought of a phrase he'd used in his books, describing soldiers who had experienced fierce combat: "thousand-yard stare."

The blush still tickled Aphra's cheeks. "My sister. She keeps trying to set me up with her husband's buddy."

"Oh, she's the matchmaker type, huh?"

"Understatement of the year. And both Di and this guy, Tony, are determined to wear me down. It's really kind of funny."

Isaac shifted his gaze to Pilar, who reclined like a lioness on the tip of his boots, washing one fluffy paw. Then he said, "I wouldn't know about such goings-on. I'm an only child. Guess I'm lucky that way, huh?"

"Quite," Aphra said.

"So tell me about that Harley of yours. How long have you been riding bikes?"

"Depends on whether you mean bicycles or motorcycles. As a kid, I practically lived on a bicycle. When I was in college, I dated a guy who raced dirt bikes. After things with him went kaput, my interest in dirt bikes hung on. I got one of my own and worked my way up from there."

"It's impressive as all get-out to see a little lady like you on a Harley."

"I've had it for two years now, and it's become like an extension of my body. But you're right, there are small women who ride motor scooters or little motorcycles but who won't touch a Harley Sportster. Go figure. It isn't like it's a Road King. It requires skill and a little getting used to, that's all." Then she asked: "Do you have a bike?"

"I've got a 69 model Harley Sportster, black with spoke wheels. Fixed it up myself. I took it out for a ride just the other day. I'm more of a fall weather person, but I've got to say, breaking out the old Hog makes me appreciate spring like nothing else can."

They were turning out to have a lot in common: an affinity for writing, cats, motorcycles, and fall. "I love riding," Aphra said. "Of course, Mom and Daddy worry themselves sick. Di and Trevor give me a hard time about it, too. But hey, I figure I'll live 'til I die."

"Who's Trevor?"

"My sister's husband."

"Oh," Isaac said matter-of-factly. "Well, I don't have anybody bugging me. The ex-wife doesn't have anything to say about it, that's for sure. And Sam, my son, has a Honda Super Hawk that he rides when he takes the notion—that is, when his wife doesn't pitch too much of a fit."

My. A provocative disclosure, the "ex" which had preceded

"wife." The lining of Aphra's mouth felt like dry cotton. "I'm sorry to hear about the divorce. I assume it's recent. You were married for many years, I know."

Isaac's expression suggested that he tasted something unpleasant. "Don't be sorry. I'm not. I'm just glad I made my parole instead of being stuck with the full life sentence."

Aphra's mind spun, but she managed to reply: "Well, you know what they say. Marriage is a fine institution, but who wants to live in an institution?"

Her quip earned her a warm Isaac Lightfoot grin.

"Are you riding your Harley today?" she asked, changing the subject to mollify the acrobats in her stomach. "I'd love to see it."

"No, I've got the Scrambler today, so I could bring that notebook to you, and also because–" He broke off and looked at his watch. "Oh hell, I've lost track of the time." He gently disengaged Pilar from his boots and stood up. "I'm sorry, but I've got to beat feet. A friend of mine is coming to town, and I don't want to be late picking him up at the airport. He was part of my recon team in 'Nam – my old KCS, Hieu. He's been living in Wisconsin, but he'll probably be staying with me for a while. We haven't seen each other in two years."

"KCS?"

"Kit Carson Scout. Former NVA or VC who served with American units. Good ones, like Hieu, gave us lots of useful input on NVA tactics."

"Oh, I remember. You wrote about them in *The Lion and the Cobra*. Well, I wouldn't want you to be late." Aphra stood, too. "I hate that you have to go, though. I've enjoyed talking with you."

He looked down at her. "Me too."

"I'll get going on that Web site."

"Don't hurry on my account."

"Meow," Pilar said, looking reproachfully up at Isaac.

He hunkered down to stroke her. "Catch you later, fuzzball."

Aphra followed Isaac out of her condo and into the April sunshine. He favored his left leg ever so slightly. He'd been badly wounded in Vietnam which had led to a medical discharge from the Army before his third tour was up, though Aphra didn't know how he'd been wounded.

It was a quiet Sunday afternoon; no one was around but the two of them. Aphra glanced toward the visitor's parking lot which was adjacent to the building she lived in. Isaac's Scrambler, its tan top removed, was parked next to Aphra's gold '67 VW Beetle, which she called the Scarab. Wilbur, her Hog, lived in her garage.

Isaac squinted against the sun then looked at Aphra, and she noticed, again, the slight—and sexy—asymmetry of his eyes. "Your hair is so pretty," he said. "It looks red, seeing it in the sunshine. Like autumn's breath burning down your back."

Startled, Aphra didn't know how to respond. She was his Web site designer, his faithful reader and fan, and that was all. Wasn't it? Okay, he liked the way her hair looked in the sun. It needn't stop his world from spinning on its axis. He was a war hero and a critically acclaimed writer, twenty years her senior. She was—what?

An admirer. A wannabe.

And he looked ill-at-ease again.

She didn't want to worsen his discomfiture or her own, so she needed to say something. "That's a lovely simile. You should use it in your next novel." Oh, what a clod she was. Divine power of the universe, help her: she was sinking. "Autumn is my favorite season, too," she added. Lamely.

"We ought to take a ride together sometime," he said. "On our bikes."

Was it a rhetorical statement or a concrete suggestion? Taking a chance that it was the latter, she replied, "I'd like that."

He nodded and headed toward his Scrambler.

On impulse, she called to him. "Isaac!"

He turned. "Yeah?"

"Have you seen *Shimmering Seascape*? You know, the movie about World War II that won all those awards last year. If you've seen it, what did you think of it?"

He scowled. "I saw about twenty minutes of it and couldn't stand any more. It's sickening. I'd dig my eyeballs out with a spoon before I'd watch five more minutes of that crap."

"I thought so." She flashed him a thumbs-up signal.

He grinned, then got into his Scrambler. Aphra returned to her condo and settled herself on the loveseat in the same spot where Isaac had sat. It was still warm and she felt oddly snug.

Was it a product of her besotted mind that Isaac Lightfoot, of all people, was attracted to more than just her Web site design talents?

4. Weekly Oinkfest

Aphra sat at Palazzo Pizzeria with Di, Trevor, and Tony, and all she could think about was going home, firing up her computer, and seeing if she'd received an e-mail from Isaac. Over the week and a half since he'd brought her the text and pictures for his Web site, she'd not only been working on the site but also engaging in e-mail conversations with him, up to three messages apiece per night, neither of them going to bed until three or four in the morning and always wishing each other a good sleep.

Who had got chatty first, Aphra or Isaac? She didn't remember. They'd worked their way from "I came up with a nifty color scheme" and "Which photo did you pick to use on the splash page?" to "Pilar took a catnap on your notebook today—I think she's still captivated by your smell" and "Consider yourself warned: if you continue to present yourself as such an endlessly fascinating young woman, you'll wind up as a character in my next novel"; yet Aphra was unable to pinpoint the mechanisms of their progression.

Her stomach-hunger was competitive with her Isaac-hunger, however, and a late supper at Palazzo Pizzeria was an excellent way to satisfy the former urge. Palazzo Pizzeria, which Aphra and Di had discovered when they were in college, had the best pizza in town—no small feat in Knoxville, a city that had, within its municipal limits, a profusion of pizza joints equal to the number of coffee stirrers that Pilar killed over the course of one year. Since Di and Trevor had started dating five years ago, they went there most Wednesday nights for what they called their Weekly Oinkfest, and they often asked Aphra to join them. But it irritated Aphra that this evening, for the first time and without telling her, they'd brought Tony, too. He sat next to her on the side of the booth that faced the salad bar, hemming her in.

They'd given the waitress their order—one large pizza with pepperoni, sausage, extra cheese, and a thin crust, and one large pizza with green peppers, olives, and a medium crust. Aphra preferred the meat-laden, fat-saturated pizza. She had an excellent metabolism, and watching her cholesterol and fat intake was one of those things she told herself she'd do soon; nonetheless, she permitted "soon" to feel comfortably far-removed when faced with a feast of this magnitude. Alas, her besieged arteries. She'd be kind to them someday.

She glanced at her watch. It was a quarter to ten. Isaac didn't send her his first message of the evening until Hieu went to bed, but Hieu might have turned in early tonight.

"So Alf," Di said with a sly smile, "how's Isaac Lightfoot's Web site going?"

"Very well," Aphra said, cobbling together a blasé face. "Actually, he's coming over Saturday to test-drive the beta version. He might want to make a few changes."

She hadn't discussed with Di her burgeoning friendship with Isaac. Why not? She didn't know. As far as Di was concerned, Aphra and Isaac were friendly associates and nothing more: client and service provider, critically acclaimed author and ardent fan. But what were they, truly? Maybe Aphra hadn't shared with Di what she and Isaac were because she wasn't sure herself.

Neither did Di know the extent of the plans Aphra and Isaac had made for the upcoming weekend. Aphra hoped the weather Saturday afternoon would be more pleasant than it was tonight or they'd get waterlogged riding their motorcycles.

"That Web site has been eating you alive," Di said. "I was surprised you wanted to come with us tonight. You can't stay holed up with those cats all the time, you know."

"Why not? My cats don't nag at me the way you do."

Di wrinkled her nose. "Liar, they do so. What about when Santiago swats your ankles when you're slow scooping his poop? What about when Pilar wants her treats?"

"It's different."

"How?"

"My cats speak Meowish, not English. Nagging is so much more pleasant in Meowish than it is in English."

"You would think so," Di said. "More and more, I think you're a cat in a human suit."

"I don't think I am, I know I am."

"Who's Isaac Lightfoot?" Tony asked.

"A local writer," Trevor said.

"Tony, if you want to hang around Alf, you're going to have to brush up on your reading," Di said.

"I've never been much of a reader," Tony said. "It was all I could do to finish books for school."

"Well," Trevor said, "as a language arts teacher, I try to read a wide range of stuff so I'll sound halfway intelligent to my fifth graders. But I've never been able to get into Isaac Lightfoot's books."

"How come?" Aphra asked.

"Don't get me wrong, I like the guy, from what I know about him. But I just can't get excited about war books, his or anybody else's. They all read the same to me. Dry as dust."

Aphra would bet her left hand that Trevor hadn't read a single book Isaac Lightfoot wrote, and she was left-handed. "He deals with many kinds of situations, not just war. He's a master of dark humor. And he's relentless when it comes to digging under the pat surfaces of things, down to the levels where the truth lives. In our formulaic time, he's downright refreshing."

Trevor laughed. "Call off your sister, Di, or she's going to sharpen her claws on my leg."

"How does this Lightfoot guy know so much about war if he's only a writer?" Tony asked. "Is he, like, an armchair quarterback? I mean, an armchair general?"

"Not hardly," Aphra said. "He's a combat veteran. He knows about war up close and personal."

"He was a Ranger, wasn't he?" Trevor asked.

"Yep. Company L, 75th Infantry, Long Range Reconnaissance Patrol." Glancing at Tony, Aphra added, "He fought in Vietnam."

"Oh," Tony said thoughtfully. "He's an old guy then."

"He might be older, but he can kick your ass," Trevor told Tony, whose face could illustrate the dictionary definition of "woebegone." "He's tougher than a pine knot. They interview him sometimes on the Public Broadcasting Channel."

"Well, I feel sorry for poor, moonstruck Alf," Di said.

"Why?" Tony asked.

"Because after she finishes up Isaac Lightfoot's Web site, she'll have to go back to admiring him from afar. Even if he weren't way too old for her, he's spoken for. Been married for decades, I guess. He's got a grown kid and everything. Probably grandchildren, too."

At her words, Tony brightened, and Aphra glared at Di. Stop encouraging him, she wanted to say. She'd also love to tell Di that Isaac was no longer married, but she was reluctant to say anything to fuel Di's resolve or her curiosity. Aphra hated being put on the spot.

Ah yes. Saved by pizza. Their chubby-cheeked teen waitress succeeded in transporting two massive pizzas to their booth, and they wasted no time digging in. Di and Trevor partook of the lower-lipid pizza while Aphra and Tony scarfed down the artery clogger. They had the same taste in pizza, if not in much else.

Which reminded Aphra. "Thanks for leaving *Shimmering Seascape* on my doorstep last night. I've been killed by work lately."

"No problem," Tony said. "I think it's funny how, even though you work at home, you're always so busy. Makes me glad to have my job at the post office. I never have to work a second over quitting time."

"But I love what I do, and besides, I get to decide my own quitting time."

Briefly he looked flummoxed, then he gave an easy shrug. "Anyway, thanks for lending me the movie. I loved it."

"I thought you would." She wished Isaac were there so she could wink at him.

A moment passed, then Tony said, around his pizza: "You know, I thought about joining the Army after high school graduation." He didn't offer anything more.

"So?" Aphra finally asked. "Why didn't you?"

"Mom didn't want me to."

She considered asking him if he were joking, but she was too afraid he wasn't.

Toward the end of the meal, Di jumped up with her hand clamped over her mouth and skedaddled in the direction of the ladies' room. Alarmed, Aphra glanced at Trevor.

"Morning sickness," he explained. "Morning sickness at night."

When Di returned to the booth, her face was the color of chalk. "I'm coming up on three months pregnant, so this should stop soon, thank goodness."

"You guys had better go home," Aphra said.

"Soon," Di said weakly. "I want to sit tight for a few minutes and drink the rest of my pop. It'll help my stomach settle."

"Junior's been making life hard for his momma." Trevor took a swig of iced tea then coughed explosively.

"Listen to you," Di said as she whacked him on the back. "How do you know it's a he, oh Great Swami? Maybe it's a she."

When Trevor could speak again, he said, "If it's a she, I hope she looks like you."

"No, no. I want her to have your big, brown, cocker-spaniel eyes. But wait, if we have a little girl who has your eyes, it'll be that much harder for me to tell her 'no' when she's being naughty..."

Oh, my. They were starting the baby talk. And Aphra had a place to go and a person to write. She looked at her watch. Hieu would surely be in bed by eleven. By the time she'd driven home, there could be a message from Isaac waiting. The thought spurred her like hot coal shoved under her butt.

"I'm going to head home," Aphra said. "I've got things I need to do."

Looking disappointed, Tony scooted out of the booth so she could do the same. "Don't you want to wait for a doggie bag?"

"You keep the rest. I don't think my cats would appreciate a doggie bag."

"Those cats of yours," Di said. "They rule the roost, don't they?"

In six months time, Di would find out what it truly meant to have a small creature ruling her roost. Aphra's cats wouldn't be able to hold a candle.

Impulsively, Aphra stooped down to hug her. "I hope you feel better soon. Make that man of yours give you a back rub."

As Aphra left Palazzo Pizzeria, the rain was falling in torrents. She got into her Scarab, her conveyance of choice for when biking was impractical, cold, or unduly soggy.

The first thing she did on arriving home was to kiss both her cats' furry noggins. The second thing she did was to fire up her computer and start her e-mail program. And the third thing she did was to lean back in her office chair and sigh with pleasure when she saw that the Sender field for one of the messages in her Inbox read "Isaac W. Lightfoot."

5. To Valhalla

Aphra and Isaac, braving the volatile currents of steel-encrusted conformists, rode like Valkyries on route to Valhalla bearing to Odin the spirit of the open road. They paused along the way to fortify themselves with hamburgers, then they spurned the claustrophobia of in-town traffic to embrace the expanse of Oak Ridge Highway.

Before embarking on their motorcycle ride, Isaac took his Web site for a trial run from Aphra's condo. He suggested no changes whatsoever and declared it to be flawless, down to the tiniest detail.

That had never happened with a client before.

But Aphra had never been on a glorious spring day motorcycle ride with a client, either.

As he'd promised, Isaac had paid her well for her Web services. Too well, considering she felt it was he who had done her the favor. She was disappointed that, excepting occasional updates to his site, their working relationship would soon be over: she was to upload his site tomorrow morning after completing the final tasks tonight. But she believed—she hoped—they'd formed a sustainable friendship.

Isaac signaled a left turn, and she followed him onto a narrow, winding road that put a damper on their speed. He had told her to beware of chugholes, and now she saw why: some of the holes were patched with tar, but many weren't. The road was flanked by meadows that were dotted with farmhouses and ringed by fences behind which loitered cud-munching cows. The cars and trucks were older and more rugged than those she was used to seeing in the suburbs of West Knoxville, and here and there a motorcycle was parked in a gravelly driveway. They'd almost arrived at Isaac's house in Solway, a small community on the outskirts of Knoxville, about twenty-five minutes away from where Aphra lived.

He wanted Aphra to meet his ball python.

She couldn't think of anyone, save Isaac, for whom she'd willingly make the acquaintance of a snake.

Isaac slowed down some more and signaled another left. Then they were on his driveway, a hard-packed dirt trail which angled to the right a hundred yards up to a tidy log cabin which was swathed by woods. They parked their bikes behind Isaac's Scrambler, removed their helmets, and secured them on their helmet locks.

From where Aphra stood, not another building could be seen. If she strained, she could hear a dog barking and a car motor rumbling in the distance. But only if she strained.

Now this was living.

She smiled at Isaac, who was taking off his windbreaker. "Not a strip mall or a red light in sight," she remarked.

"This is where I grew up. People can breathe here without sucking another person up his nose."

The sleeveless black shirt he wore revealed a tattoo on his strapping right arm. Though the tattoo was somewhat faded, its image remained clear: it was the coiled rattlesnake from the Revolutionary War-era Gadsden Flag, under which was inscribed "Don't Tread on Me."

He saw her looking at his tattoo and said, "Relic of my Vietnam years. I got it on my first tour. The guy who did it didn't speak or read a word of English. He copied a picture I had."

"I like it." Indeed, it suited him. Aphra lifted her gaze to meet his, but she soon found herself looking at his tattoo again. It was nowhere near as overwhelming as his eyes. She was seized by a compulsion to touch the tattoo, to trace its outlines, to see if his skin felt as warm as it looked.

So Isaac couldn't see her sudden, fierce blush, she turned toward Wilbur, removed her suede jacket, and ordered her cheeks to cool. A breeze gusted full on her face, which helped, but when she lay her jacket carefully across the seat of her bike and moved away, she saw Isaac crossing the flagstone walkway that led to his front door. He glanced over his shoulder and gestured to Aphra.

"Come on in."

She'd follow Isaac Lightfoot into the ninth circle of Dante's

Hell.

Fortunately, however, his home was more hospitable than *Inferno* by countless orders of magnitude.

The first word that came to mind as she entered his cabin and looked around was "spacious." The cabin was comprised of one large room, and its ceiling was high. There was a sole walled enclave, likely the bathroom, beside which was an Army cot and a small bed.

The rightmost wall of the cabin was lined by bookshelves. Situated along this wall, too, was an office area: a leather chair, walnut desk, computer system and a printer. Next to the computer monitor, there was a framed photograph of a young man and a young woman, presumably Isaac's son and daughter-in-law. Dappled in sunshine and grinning widely, they were posed in front of Isaac's cabin with their arms linked. Also on the desk was an aquarium where a plump, black and tan-patterned snake basked on shredded bark substrate under a heat lamp.

The left side of the cabin was taken up by a kitchen, complete with a refrigerator, cabinets, a table, and four chairs.

"I like that you have so few interior walls," Aphra said.

"Walls are over-rated," Isaac replied. "I built this place myself, and I wasn't settling for any less than exactly the way I wanted it."

Not a scrap of carpet could be found in the cabin. Instead, Isaac had placed woven rugs over the gleaming hardwood flooring. The largest of the rugs was positioned in front of a fireplace, and sitting atop the rug were two burgundy leather wingback chairs with a reading lamp and an end table between them.

And oh, Isaac's fireplace, extra-wide, constructed of large, gray stones! In early May it was pristine, the stack of logs within untouched by flame, but it had to be heavenly on chilly winter nights. Aphra moved closer to the fireplace for a better view and imagined Isaac splitting logs to fuel it, a vision that directed her attention to the mantle above—a massive beam of rough-hewn oak.

Hanging centered over the mantle was an authentic flintlock Tennessee Long Rifle with rust and scanty brown color on its barrel. Its stock was well-worn with time's dents and scratches, and the wood in its grip was darkened. On the left side of the rifle was a copy of the surrender document signed by General Cornwallis, presented in an ornately carved pewter frame, and on the right side was a copy of the Declaration of Independence, presented in a humble wooden frame. One object rested on Isaac's mantle, centered under the flintlock rifle: a rusty, dented, and obviously genuine tin cup.

The tableau called to Aphra's mind *On Self-Reliance*, a non-fictional work written by Isaac about the decline of individual self-sufficiency in modern America and the vital role of self-sufficiency in preserving a free society. She'd read *On Self-Reliance* for the first time during her junior year of high school, and taking its wisdom to heart on the personal level helped her garner enough dignity, for the remainder of her sentence to purgatory, to hold herself more boldly harmless from high school's unique brand of tyranny. It was amazing how a book could resonate on such different levels of meaning for a thirty-three year-old than for a seventeen year-old.

"The fireplace symbolizes personal independence," Isaac said. Lost in her thoughts, Aphra hadn't heard him come up behind her. "The rifle, with its marks of use, symbolizes the means by which freedom is won and maintained. The Cornwallis document symbolizes the fall of tyranny, and its fancy frame represents the glitter of tyranny that masks defeat. The Declaration of Independence symbolizes the courage needed to be free, and its plain frame emphasizes the significance of the document in its own right. The opulence of tyrants, after all, can never match the simple beauty of freedom."

"No copy of the Constitution?" Aphra asked.

"Nope. The agreement of men to govern isn't as important as the declaration of one's freedom."

"What about the tin cup?" She turned around to face him.

"It's a symbol of the sacrifice required by people to be free."

"Spoken like a true soldier," she said.

"A free person has a responsibility to other free people, as well as to those people who will come after. If you're not willing to fight to maintain the freedom you have today, you condemn those in the future of a life of servitude. Inside every free person must reside the heart of a soldier."

In her examination of Isaac's hearth, Aphra glimpsed his heart. And she liked what she saw.

"Tell me about the rifle." She recalled from Isaac's Web site that he collected and rebuilt antique and military surplus rifles.

"It belonged to an ancestor of mine, who fought in the Revolutionary War, and it's been handed down all the generations since. Quite a few of us Lightfoot men have been veterans. My great-great grandpa fought in the Civil War, my grandpa fought in World War I, and as you know, my daddy was a World War II vet."

"I'm good at shooting a rifle," Aphra said. "I tried the Girl Scouts when I was a kid, but I hated it. A brownie is a dessert, not a human. They never did anything fun. My best neighborhood buddy was a Boy Scout, so I started hanging around with his troop instead. I became an honorary Boy Scout, and I kicked the boys' butts in their rifle competitions."

Isaac smiled at her. "That's what I like to hear." He nudged her toward his desk. "Now, let me introduce you to King Leonidas."

He'd assured Aphra the snake was well-contained. And it wasn't very large—looked to be about six feet in length. With Isaac nearby, she wasn't frightened.

Well, not inordinately so.

But here was something Aphra didn't expect: the snake's pattern was stunning. The tan portion had an iridescent green cast, and the black portion gleamed like onyx. The snake was motionless except for its tongue, which flicked out as Aphra watched.

"He's beautiful," she said. "I guess I didn't expect a snake to be so pretty."

Isaac smiled. "Be careful. You'll give him a big head."

"What does he eat?"

"Mice. I get them at the pet store out on the main highway. Fed him one just the other day, so he won't need to eat again for about a week and a half."

"How long have you had him?"

"Three years or so. I got him to keep the ex-wife from sniffing around my cabin."

Aphra laughed; she couldn't help it.

"And I'm fond of him, too. He's a fascinating critter. When I write or do research, he coils around my arm. He's real easygoing and likes my warmth. I feel sorry for the mice he eats, but it's nature, and snakes have got to eat, too."

So Isaac's ex-wife was afraid of snakes? Then Aphra wouldn't be. Nervous, perhaps, but not afraid.

"Um, Isaac? Do you think King Leonidas would like to coil around my arm?"

He chuckled. "Sure he would. Have you ever held a snake before?"

Aphra shook her head, and Isaac said: "Just be sure and support him good. He doesn't like to dangle. I'll get him out then hand him to you."

Turning up her courage knob, Aphra reminded herself that she was seldom adverse to a new adventure and replied with a hearty, "Yup!"

Isaac removed the snake from the aquarium, holding him with both hands: one hand near the snake's head and the other hand supporting its lower body. Aphra touched the snake, putting her hands where Isaac had put his, though not quite touching his fingers. When she had hold of the snake, Isaac coiled the rest of its length around her forearm. She was surprised at the feel of the snake: it was dry and its belly smooth, not the least bit slimy. Why had she thought a snake would be slimy? It seemed silly now.

Isaac's gaze was warm behind his eyeglasses, and Aphra had to return her gaze to King Leonidas, who had tightened ever-so-slightly around her forearm.

"You're something else. I've never met a woman quite like you before." Isaac's rumbly baritone was gentle.

And Aphra would be hard-pressed to hide her glow of satisfaction.

"So does your ex-wife come around here much?" she asked. She was uncomfortable with the idea of meeting Isaac's ex. Why? Because she was hopelessly gooey-eyed over Isaac, of course.

Poor Alf, Di would say. Cuddling with snakes to impress your hero.

"She doesn't come around much now," Isaac said. "When we first divorced, though, going on four years ago, she did. And for a while, telling her to quit did no good at all. She'd borrow stuff whenever she could, just barge in like she owned the place, with me sitting here like a big-assed bird. Let's just say I got in the habit of locking my doors, even when I was home."

"That's rude," Aphra said, "but I've heard of other people like that, who divorced after many years of marriage. It's as though their separate homes are offshoots of their old, familiar household.

Especially when they share kids, grandkids or whatever."

"Yeah, I've seen that, too, but I think it's dumb. In my book, divorce means divorce. Or it ought to. Just like marriage ought to mean marriage."

Aphra heard a vehicle in Isaac's driveway, and as the door opened, she thought, oh shit, it's his ex-wife. But thank goodness it wasn't. It was a man with wiry, corded muscles and graying dark hair. He was short, over a head shorter than Isaac and only an inch or two taller than Aphra. His right cheek was branded by a patch of lumpy scar tissue that was at least three inches long. She'd forgotten about Hieu. He carried two plastic grocery bags in each lean, sharp-knuckled hand.

"Hello, Snake. I'm glad you're back." Hieu spoke in a smooth tenor, and his Vietnamese accent rendered his voice strangely reminiscent of wind chimes. "Whose purple motorcycle—" He stopped short when he saw Aphra. "What a lovely young lady. Is this a friend of Sam and Cheryl?"

A scowl flitted across Isaac's face, but as soon as she noticed it, it disappeared. "No, buddy. This is my friend I told you I was seeing today. Aphra. Remember?"

Hieu's grin could split his face. "Oh, yes. I apologize. You and Isaac are motorcycle friends, then?"

"And python friends, too, it would seem," Aphra said. She handed King Leonidas back to Isaac, who put him back in his aquarium.

"Aphra, this is Hieu, also known as Swamp Rat or Swampy. My oldest friend."

Hieu shook his finger at Isaac but his gaze was still on Aphra. "I'm not so old. You, either."

"Fifty-three's not old, is it?" Isaac said with a sigh. "And sixty's getting younger every day." He took the grocery bags from Hieu, carried them to the kitchen, and began stowing items in the refrigerator and the cabinets. Hieu and Aphra followed. Hieu was light on his feet, like a ballet dancer.

"Thanks for picking up the groceries," Isaac said to Hieu.

"You're welcome. You'll be happy to see that they had the hot peanuts today. And it's good to meet you, Aphra. Isaac says you're designing a fine Web site for him."

"I hope so. It's nice to meet you, too. I've heard a lot about you."

"Only good things, I hope." Hieu took a seat at the kitchen table, and Aphra joined him.

"Oh, Snake," Hieu said. "Before I forget: Sam called you as I was leaving to go to the store. He wants you to call him back on his cellular phone."

"I bet he's wanting to borrow a tool." Isaac shook his head. "I swear, he's got to have half my tools in his garage by now."

Hieu looked sad. "Children can be difficult, but I miss mine."

From Isaac's e-mails, Aphra recalled that Hieu and his wife had separated and that she was refusing to let him have contact even by telephone with their children: a boy and a girl, ages eight and ten. Hieu's wife had come to the United States from Vietnam with him twelve years ago. And last month, after Hieu was laid off from his job, she had thrown him out of their house in Wisconsin.

Isaac retrieved a cell phone that was charging on the kitchen table. He punched in a number and waited. Then he said, "Hey there, son. Uncle Hieu said you called. I was riding my bike ... Well, that's fine, you can borrow my wire feed welder, but I'll need it back sometime, okay? Do you want to pick it up today? Yeah, hop on by and get it. Where are you? Okay. We'll be here." He put the phone down and joined Aphra and Hieu at the table. "Sam and Cheryl are over at Momma's. They'll be here in about ten minutes."

So Aphra would meet Isaac's son today. She wondered what he'd be like. And she wondered what he'd think of her.

6. Cocky Cartoon Rabbit

Isaac's son came into the cabin accompanied not by one woman, but by two. The lanky blonde didn't look a day over twenty. Aphra studied the other one, a heavily made-up woman with chin-length hair the color of bronze. Isaac had said that Sam and Cheryl were visiting Isaac's mother, but Isaac's mother would have to be in her seventies. The bronze-haired woman looked to be around Isaac's age. A sister, perhaps? No, Isaac had said he was an only child.

A nasty hunch took shape, which solidified when Hieu said, "Hello, Norma. I haven't seen you in a long time." He seemed uncomfortable. Perhaps he wished the long time had lasted much, much longer.

"A very long time." Norma turned toward Isaac as if to banish Hieu from her sight. "I hope you don't mind me coming along with the kids. We were eating supper over at your momma's, and it would have been out of the way for them to take me home."

Aphra wanted to be out of the way. Alas, terraforming had yet to begin on Mars. When she shifted in her chair, three pairs of eyeballs locked their gazes on her. If a paramecium had a limbic system, it would feel, under the scrutiny of the scientist's microscope, much the way Aphra felt now.

Isaac rubbed his beard distractedly. "Aphra, this is my son, Sam, and my daughter-in-law, Cheryl." His voice sounded oddly flat. "And this is Sam's mother, Norma. Sam, Cheryl, Norma, this is my friend, Aphra Porter."

"Hi," she volunteered.

Sam and Cheryl said hello, but Norma only stared at Aphra. Sam took a seat at the table between Isaac and Hieu.

"Wait, Sammy," Norma said. "Before you get settled, get me your father's office chair so I can sit down, too. I don't want to get any closer to that god-awful snake than I am right now. That thing scares me to death."

Sam retrieved Isaac's office chair and rolled it into the kitchen. Norma took it from him, positioned it about a foot away from Isaac, and sat down. Her strong perfume assaulted Aphra's nose like a solvent, so she turned in her chair, angling herself away from Isaac and Norma, seeking relief.

Then Sam sat back down. He was a fresh-faced, gangly young man who, Aphra guessed, was in his early twenties. His eagerness to please his mother reminded her of Tony. Cheryl, in a yellow maternity dress that bulked around her thin body, stood behind Sam and rubbed her still-small belly.

Norma looked Aphra's way again. How different they were from each other—Aphra with her long, loose hair, blue jeans and black duty boots; Norma with her strappy high heels, hot pink pantsuit, and inch-long hot pink nails. With nails like those, how could she do anything with her hands? Isaac had been married to Norma for a quarter-century. Was this what he liked in women?

"You're Isaac's friend, huh?" Norma said. "How did y'all meet?"

Aphra and Isaac answered at the same time.

"I met him at a book signing."

"She's redoing my Web site."

They exchanged glances, and Aphra gestured for him to reply. She wanted his ex-wife's attention off her, if only for a second or two.

"We met at my most recent book signing," he said. "Aphra's a heck of a good Web site designer, so I hired her to redo my site."

"Oh, book signings," Norma said. "How well I remember. They were something, weren't they? All those fans. Always made me glad I wasn't the writer of the family because I could just sit back and hang in the background. Remember the book signing in Atlanta back years ago when Sammy was playing with his toy trucks under your desk? He was so cute."

"I remember," Isaac grumbled. "I also remember I tried to get you to take him back to the hotel because he was tired and grumpy."

"I look forward to seeing our grandchild playing under your desk at a future book signing," Norma said, as though Isaac hadn't spoken. "Won't that be a treat?"

"I'm working on it, Momma Lightfoot," Cheryl said. "He or she's baking in my oven right now."

"That's a cool Hugger out there, Dad," Sam said. "Did you get another bike?"

"No, son. It's Aphra's."

Sam stared at Aphra. "Wow. I've never met a woman who rides a Harley before."

She opened her mouth to reply, but Norma spoke to him first, grinning like a cocky cartoon rabbit. "I guess being one of your father's fans and all, Abra got her a Harley because she read somewhere about how much he likes them. Your father always did have a way with his women fans." Her front teeth stood out like tombstones.

"I'm sorry, I don't mean to be rude," Aphra said, "but until last week, I had no idea that Isaac rides a Harley. And my name isn't Abra. It's Aphra. Short for Aphrodite." As soon as it was out of her mouth, Aphra regretted what she'd said, but the name elicited no recognition from Norma, only blankness. Mythology must not be one of Norma's strong subjects.

"I'd be scared to death to get on one of them bikes." Still rubbing her belly, Cheryl gazed at Aphra as though Aphra were newly arrived from an extra-galactic planet.

"Abra, how about you give your chair to Cheryl?" Norma suggested. "She's pregnant and needs the rest."

If Norma truly cared about Cheryl's delicate condition, then why didn't she have Sam get Isaac's office chair for Cheryl instead of taking it herself? Oh well, outsiders shouldn't be doubters. Aphra started to get up, but Isaac spoke before she could do so.

"I'll get that welder, Sam, and put it in your truck. Cheryl, you take my chair."

Isaac left the cabin and Cheryl co-opted his chair. Alone with Isaac's family, Aphra found the air fraught with silence, and she sought comfort in the wood grain pattern of the table.

Hieu saved her. "So Sam, my man. How's it dangling?"

Sam clapped him on the back. "I think you mean 'How's it hanging,' Uncle Hieu."

"Oh, dear," Hieu said. "The death of me will be American idioms."

Sam laughed and Cheryl giggled, her hand over her mouth.

"Which would you prefer, a son or a daughter?" Hieu tossed out the question for either of the younger Lightfoots—Lightfeet?—to catch.

"As long as it's human, we don't care," Sam said good-naturedly. "But we'll probably name it after Grandpa or Granny Ellis. That's what Momma wants. Isn't it, Momma?"

Norma nodded approvingly.

And Sam was reminding Aphra even more of Tony. Before being granted leave from Norma's court, was Sam required to kiss one of her gaudy rings? Perhaps he bowed and curtsied, hoping for a brush from the hem of her pantsuit in blessing.

"Have you met Isaac's mother yet?" Her Holiness asked Aphra.

"Isaac's mother? No. Why would I? I'm not designing a Web site for her."

Norma tittered, oblivious to Aphra's sarcasm. "Of course not. She can't even turn on a computer. She's a great old lady, though. And a wonderful cook. My own momma is dead, and all Miss Maggie has in the world is Isaac, me, and our kids. Me and Miss Maggie are close as can be. Do you know, she still calls me her daughter-in-law?"

"How nice for you both." Aphra felt nauseated. Maybe those hamburgers had been greasier than she'd thought. "I'd say you two have known each other for a long time."

"Going on thirty years. Longer than you've been on this earth, I'm sure."

"I'm thirty-three," Aphra said, which didn't help much. Why did everything she say make things worse? Her arms felt like a pretzel knotted across her chest, and her face was a mask. Underneath the mask, she longed to go home to her cats: her warm, fuzzy family. She didn't belong here.

Isaac came back in. "Okay, son, that welder's in your truck, ready to go." He emphasized the word "go." Sam and Cheryl duly got up, but Norma stayed put.

"Come on, Momma," Sam said. "Let's get rolling."

Norma rose reluctantly, looking at Isaac, but his gaze was on Sam and Cheryl. "Catch y'all later," he said to them.

"Bye, everybody," Sam said. "Thanks for lending me the welder, Dad." He and Cheryl headed out.

"Call me next week," Norma murmured conspiratorially to

Isaac once Sam and Cheryl were out of earshot. "Our baby boy's got a special birthday later on this month, you know. The big two-five. I'd like us to throw a surprise birthday party for him." Before Isaac could respond, she scooted out of the cabin and shut the door with a thud.

Isaac removed his eyeglasses, put his head in his hands, and rubbed his temples.

"Is there a real-life infiltration of the body grabbers going on here?" Hieu asked, looking befuddled. "Like in that old black and white movie we watched last night? Norma was acting—not like Norma. At least not like the Norma I remember."

Isaac shook his head. "I don't want to talk about it."

"I'm sorry, Snake." Hieu looked at him sympathetically. "Women are from hell."

Aphra stood up, feigned a stretch. "Well, I need to head home. I'll upload your site tomorrow morning, Isaac. Check it out and let me know if you find anything you want me to tweak. And I'm available for updates whenever you need them."

Hieu looked taken aback, and Isaac looked alarmed.

"I didn't mean to offend," Hieu said. "I didn't mean you were from hell."

So Norma was a woman, and she, Aphra, wasn't. Nobody believed she was a woman. And who cared? All she wanted was to sit in her La-Z Girl and cuddle with Santiago and Pilar. She knew that Isaac had come to care about her after a fashion. But evidently, she'd misinterpreted a lot. She'd been a fool, and she'd only hurt herself. Her crush on Isaac had turned into a sword, and she'd cut her hands fondling the blade.

Time to drop the sword.

"I enjoyed our ride, but I've got cats to feed and poop to scoop. But if you like, we'll go for another bike ride sometime. And take care, Hieu." She was surprised she sounded strong. Perhaps it was because she knew she could cry all she wanted when she got home. Her cats would understand. They were the only ones who could.

She turned to make her exodus but was stopped when a big hand, warm and rough-palmed, closed around her upper arm and made her flesh tingle.

"It's dark," Isaac said huskily. He'd put his glasses back on. "Let me follow you home. See that you make it back all right."

She turned to face him, and his hand dropped from her arm. "You don't need to. I'm used to riding Wilbur at night. I told you about my late night rides in our e-mail talks, didn't I?"

"Yeah, you did, but I want to do this. Please let me." His eyes were strange. He made Aphra think of a lion in a concrete box, soundproofed to the outer world, who was reluctant to roar lest the sound burst his eardrums.

She nodded. Maybe he'd left something at her condo. Of course. The notebook. He would want it back. With it were several of his pictures.

Aphra and Isaac put on their jackets and helmets, mounted their bikes, turned their keys and hit their starters. Their Harley V-twins vibrated to life, ready to propel them to their common destination. Too bad it was the end of their line.

Aphra rode ahead, and Isaac followed. The traffic was sparse in Solway, but it picked up once they reached the outskirts of West Knoxville, and by the time they closed in on Cedar Bluff, where Aphra lived, typical Saturday evening malfunction junction was in full-swing. Though twenty-five minutes ago she couldn't get away quickly enough, she found herself missing the quiet of Isaac's cabin and the surrounding countryside. She stopped at a red light, touched her feet down, leaned on her handlebars, and reflected.

Before the entrance of Isaac's family—Norma entrenched in "family," it would seem—Aphra had got the impression, from their tête-à-tête over King Leonidas, that Isaac was divorced from his ex-wife in all senses of the word. Maybe he wished it were so. But it wasn't. Norma wouldn't have it like that. Not now. She must have seen the way Aphra looked at him. It had showed in Aphra's eyes, set off the starting gun, and Norma was off.

But Norma overestimated Aphra's willingness to run the race. Aphra didn't run races she couldn't win. Isaac and Norma had a history. They shared a son. Aphra was Isaac's fan. A groupie. A service provider-come-buddy, and that was all. With bitterness, Aphra recalled how Isaac emphasized her service provider role in front of his ex-wife. Was it for his benefit or for Norma's? Could it have been for Aphra's benefit, cruel in the short term but compassionate over the long term, to keep in check any silly dreams she might harbor? Could he, too, have noticed the look in her eyes?

Aphra glanced at her rear view mirror: there was Isaac, stalled in traffic like her. Two cars separated them. She'd love to be warmed by his concern in seeing her home, but she didn't want to pick up the sword again.

The light changed to green, and she eased out Wilbur's clutch, rolled on his throttle, and moved out, on, and away. The traffic thinned in front of her, and a mile from her condominium complex, she found herself overwhelmed by the need for speed. She clicked the shifter down to third, rolled again on the throttle, and as the engine roared into life and revved high, her ever-obliging Hog rewarded her with acceleration that pulled on her arms. Freedom. Freedom of movement, freedom of will. Feelings were only feelings, and feelings could be controlled. Freedom to control oneself was freedom, too.

And she could go anywhere she wished, but she thought she'd just go home.

For the last mile of her journey, she'd avoided watching Isaac in her rear view mirror, but he must have matched her speed: he rode into the parking lot as she eased her bike into her garage. She pulled off her helmet and left it in Wilbur's seat.

Isaac caught up to Aphra on her doorstep as she plucked a stack of mail from her box. When he was in front of her, it was as though he'd lost the power of speech. He looked down at her with his face in shadow and the nearly-full moon behind. His eyes, behind the glasses, were unreadable.

She broke the silence. "I guess you'd like your notebook back."

"Notebook?" He said it like it was a word in a dying, ancient language.

"Yes, the one with your pictures."

"I'd forgotten about it."

"Would you like to come in?" Aphra couldn't help but expect him to say yes. But she was wrong.

"No, I need to get back to the house. But I'd like us to get together again sometime."

So would I, Aphra thought. Or had she said those words out loud? She wished she could see his eyes. She wanted him to e-mail her when he got back home. Should she ask him to? There could be no harm in that. They'd exchanged e-mail every night for the past two weeks, and there was no reason why it shouldn't continue.

They could be friends, no sweat, no strain. That was, as long as Aphra kept her ridiculous crush under control.

As long as she kept uppermost in mind her proper place in his life.

"Could you send me an e-mail when you got home, to let me know you made it back with no problems?" Aphra said. "The traffic in West Knoxville can be pretty rough on a Saturday night."

Shadows or no, Aphra could tell he was smiling. "I will," he said. "I sure will."

She could stand out there forever, gazing up at Isaac backlit by the moon, but faithful to her resolve, she wouldn't bow to such foolishness. Wouldn't. Couldn't. "Well, good night. If I don't get in there and start scooping poop, the whole condo complex will be reeking, and the men in the biohazard suits will be knocking on my door."

He didn't respond in kind. Instead, Aphra saw slow movement on his right side. It was his hand, which he brought up until it was touching her cheek. He stroked her face, first hesitantly then more deliberately, from her temple along her jaw to her chin. Again. And oh, as she pressed her cheek into his hand, again. His touch was tender. Reverent. Resolve? What resolve? No touch from any other person had made her feel like this. She sighed, she couldn't help herself. And she was no longer steady on her feet. This wasn't happening. It was. It wasn't.

It was.

He bent down, his bearded visage supplanting the face of the moon. From horizon to horizon, everything was Isaac. He nudged Aphra's chin upward, and his lips brushed hers. Who moved away, she or Isaac? It didn't matter, though, because their lips reconnected in an instant, and this time, neither of them moved away. She dropped her mail and her keys. They kissed cautiously, their fingertips barely touching, afraid of what they might unleash. Perhaps they had plenty of reason to be afraid: Aphra was trembling, and her blood surged with tsunamic force. When, following an interlude of timelessness, Isaac drew away from Aphra's parted lips and feathered kisses on their corners, on her forehead, and on her cheeks, she knew that she was lost, that there was no resolve, that there was no control.

There was only feeling. There was only Isaac.

From horizon to horizon.

Heaven, Elysium, Mount Olympus help her.

Aphra wanted to say, Isaac, you're leaving here with my heart in your keeping, you shall have it forevermore, you've had it for eighteen years already, though you didn't know it. Cherish it. Protect it well.

But she could say none of those things. She hadn't the breath.

"Good night, my sweet Aphra. I want to see you again soon. And I'll send you an e-mail tonight." He moved off her doorstep.

"Yes," she managed to reply as she picked up her keys and her mail. "See you soon."

Isaac Lightfoot had called her his sweet Aphra. It resounded in her ears as she went into her condo and closed the door, it resounded in her mind as she fed, cuddled, and cleaned up after her cats, and it resounded in her heart as she settled into her office chair to put the finishing touches on his Web site and wait for his e-mail.

Yes, the sword's blade was sharp, but she'd keep her hands firmly on its grip.

7. Joy as Life's Work

By one o'clock in the morning, however, Aphra was less euphoric than perplexed. She'd clicked her e-mail program's Send and Receive icon numerous times in the last five hours, pulling in forwarded jokes from both Di and the Resident Bodhisattva of East Tennessee —otherwise known as Daddy—but nothing from Isaac. A call to the Tennessee Highway Patrol confirmed that there had been no motorcycle accidents over the last twelve hours. Isaac must have made it home okay. Could he have forgotten to e-mail her? Did something else come up, waylaying him, asserting priority?

She didn't understand, but she was giving him the benefit of the doubt. After the kiss they had shared, she could do nothing less. If that kiss were meaningless to Isaac, then Aphra must forevermore distrust the efficacy of her fundamental sensory capacity, and she wasn't ready to take that step.

Pilar rubbed against her feet, which were clad in thick bedtime socks. Santiago was curled on her desk; his paw covered her trackball. Go to bed, Mom, they seemed to say. It'll be all right once you get some sleep. Who was she to ignore the sage of advice of cats?

She got in bed, and soon, Santiago made a meatloaf of himself on her hip and Pilar claimed her feet. Over and over again, Aphra relived The Kiss, and she drifted off, hoping to see Isaac in her dreams. Surely there would be an e-mail from him when she got up.

But there wasn't. She'd set her alarm for eight o'clock so she could get Isaac's site uploaded by nine. Groggily, she hauled herself into her office, fired up her computer, and opened her e-mail program. She glared at her Inbox window as though she could will into existence a message from Isaac. She saw "J. McGaha" and

"Freelance News", but no "Isaac W. Lightfoot."

She was disappointed. And stumped. And she couldn't deny that she was hurt.

She closed her e-mail program and ran her file transfer protocol application, employing the user name and password given to her by Pace & Rafferty Publishing that allowed her access to their server. Uploading Isaac's new site and re-checking it on the server was a simple procedure which she completed in twenty minutes. She opened her e-mail program again, but it refused to oblige her: still no message from Isaac. She sent him a brief missive letting him know she'd uploaded his site then closed her e-mail program with a resolute click.

The phone rang. Maybe it was Isaac. Her hand danced over and grabbed it before the second ring, but her stomach turned to lead when she heard Di's voice.

"Hiya, Alf. I was hoping you'd be up. I remembered you were going to upload Isaac Lightfoot's site this morning."

"Yeah," she said.

"What's wrong?"

"Nothing."

"Oh, there's something wrong. I can tell. Wait, I know what it is: you've got post-Isaac Lightfoot depression. I can read you like a book."

"No, you can't." Di had no idea.

"Don't bother to deny it. I've got the perfect cure, though. Come to church with me and Trevor. They're having a special musical program today. Spring Cantata Sunday. You'll like it."

"Oh, why not. Besides rearranging my sock drawer, I don't have anything else to do." Aphra had no plans to rearrange her sock drawer, and there was plenty she could do. But the prospect of getting out of the condo for a while was welcome. She could weather no more disappointment, at least not now.

"Great," Di said. "Trevor and I will pick you up at ten thirty."

Organized religion wasn't Aphra's bag, but the church Di and Trevor attended, an enormous Bible Fellowship parish, was blessed with a pipe organ, an orchestra, skilled musicians, and a seventy-five voice choir. Albert Schweitzer had once said: "There are two means of refuge from the miseries of life: music and cats."

Aphra wholeheartedly concurred.

To avoid her office and the communications devices therein, she took her time getting ready, gussying herself up as much as she ever did, though she was adamant that no pair of itchy hose should touch her legs in warm weather. She applied understated makeup, lip gloss, and a spritz of lemony perfume. And by the time she heard the doorbell, she was decked out in white pumps and a turquoise dress.

She couldn't keep her mind off Isaac, however, or off their kiss. Could one lift one's spirits by dressing up? The congregation of Trinity Fellowship, Di's church, was laid back: she could wear slacks and a blouse.

Perhaps by dressing up, she was making a statement that her Daniel Boone jacket, blue jeans, and duty boots weren't glued on, that sometimes she looked like a woman.

Trouble was, Isaac wasn't there to see.

Tony, however, was. When Aphra opened her door, there he was on the step, standing to the front of Di and Trevor as if he were being presented. His expression, surprised and beatific, revealed an erroneous belief that she'd dressed up for him.

Aphra didn't know Tony was coming. But how could she not have guessed? Her angst over Isaac rendered her oblivious to Di sticking Tony in her face every chance she got. And Aphra feared that a dab of encouragement, however unintentional, would stretch a long way with Tony.

"Wow, Alf," he said, agog. "I've never seen you in a dress before."

"It's a rare occasion," Di said, grinning. "I recommend you enjoy it."

Aphra sighed.

Di seldom looked like anything but a woman unless she looked like a daffodil, which she assuredly did today. She was wearing a dress patterned in yellow and green, white hose, and white high-heeled shoes. Her short, precision-cut hair stood in stunningly choreographed swoops and swirls, and a floral scent emanated from her neck.

Meeting Isaac's ex-wife and daughter-in-law had the pleasant side effect of helping Aphra to better appreciate her sister. Di esteemed feminine grooming, but unlike Isaac's ex, Di didn't make her appearance an all-consuming mania: Norma must spend hours of an evening excavating her facial features from the layers of makeup she heaped upon them. And unlike Cheryl, Di hadn't turned awareness of pregnancy's physical changes into an obsession, nor did she use her condition to pander for pity or attention. Di would never succumb to maternity clothing, which she deemed "goofy"—until progressive distension of her abdomen left her no other choice. Aphra expected Di to become what she'd always thought of as a "cool mom": a woman who rises to the challenges of motherhood without forgetting who she is. Cheryl, on the other hand, appeared to be headed for Mom-O-Blivion.

Aphra pitied Isaac, surrounded by such women. It made her wonder what his mother was like.

"You look right perky, Di," Aphra said. "Is the morning sickness any better?"

"The morning sickness isn't bad. It's the evening sickness that's had me eating chicken soup and crackers for supper."

"Poor sis." Aphra patted Di's head. It was something she'd done since they were little girls. And Di never fussed at Aphra for messing up her hair.

"You seem to be feeling better than you were when we spoke on the phone," Di said.

"Yeah, I guess I am."

"That's good. Lovelorn and star struck you may be, but your job for Isaac Lightfoot is finished, and you have to go on with your life."

Indeed. Why, Aphra wondered, did Isaac kiss her? Why didn't he e-mail her?

"Come on," Trevor urged. "Let's go." He and Tony looked like Fric and Frac in their slacks and short-sleeved dress shirts.

Trinity Fellowship Church of Knoxville, the congregation Trevor had been a member of since childhood, was housed in a long, low, single-story building that was made of craggy stones and crowned by a peaked roof. Tony walked by Aphra's side with Di and Trevor behind. She wished he wouldn't do that.

They entered the auditorium, an immense room painted antique white that accommodated rows and rows of wooden pews. When they found an empty pew, Tony scooted in beside Aphra as she seated herself, and Di and Trevor hung back, sliding in next to him once he was settled. Could they be any more obvious? Would

Di admit, if Aphra asked her, to having encouraged Tony further where Aphra was concerned?

Probably not.

Focusing on the service eased Aphra's impatience with Tony's attentions. The sermon, *Joy as Life's Work*, was eloquent and inspired—though she wished she felt more joyful—but it was the music that moved her most: J. S. Bach's Cantata 129 sung in English, *Awake Thou, Wintry Earth,* which consecrated the arrival of spring with flawless vocal harmonies, trumpet, and pipe organ. Listening to the final chorale, carried away by its transcendent swells, she thought about how Isaac's kiss had awakened her last night. Would he now have her return to sleep?

Albert Schweitzer was a wise man. By the time Aphra took leave of Trinity Fellowship along with Di and Company, she was feeling more herself. Finely crafted music, unlike life, never disappointed her with dissonance.

"Thanks, Di," Aphra said, back on her doorstep. "That was just what I needed."

"I figured. Hey, do you want to come to our place this afternoon? We thought today would be a good day to kick off Sunday cookout season. Ride on over to the house with us now, if you want. You can help me and Mom get everything together."

"I'll be there, too," Tony said, volunteering what he probably thought was an incentive.

Aphra might as well go. It would keep her from hovering over her infernal computer all afternoon. Though Pilar and Santiago would miss her, they'd understand.

"Okay, I'll come. Your macaroni is hard to beat, even with a stick. Give me a minute to change, though. I'm not wearing these pumps on your lawn."

The Meow Chorale differed from the chorale in Bach's Cantata 129, but it was no less welcome. Aphra picked up her kitties, first Pilar then Santiago, and bestowed kisses on their fuzzy heads. She was always so happy to see their sweet, whiskered faces, whether it had been five hours or five minutes since she'd last seen them.

Should she check her e-mail? What if Isaac had written? He probably hadn't. To avoid further disappointment, she spared her office only a cursory glance as she passed by on her way to the bedroom.

But wait. Something was blinking.

Aphra backtracked two steps and entered her office. It was the red light on her telephone, indicating receipt of a new call. She guessed Bodhi or the Earth Mother had called about Di's cookout. Services at their Unitarian Universalist Church were shorter than those at Trinity Fellowship. She punched in the number for her voice mail then listened.

"Aphra? Are you up? Are you home?" Isaac Lightfoot's voice rumbled into her ear. "Please check your e-mail, and call me when you can." His call came at ten-forty, five minutes after she'd left for church with Di and Company. Oh, the inhumanity!

Her computer took ages to boot up. Maybe she should leave the stupid thing on all the time. Her e-mail program took so long in starting that she wondered if it was hung, but no, there it went, and it started pulling in new messages. There was one from a local grocer whose site Aphra had designed a year ago. There was a lone piece of Spam advertising mega-vitamins. And finally, there was one delightful digital communiqué whose Sender field read "Isaac W. Lightfoot." Her hand trembled as she double-clicked the subject line: "I'M SORRY!" The message was time-stamped ten-fifteen that morning.

His message read: "I'm sorry I didn't e-mail you last night. I wanted to write you, but my hands were full dealing with an unpleasantness that gobbled up the remainder of my night. I hope you'll forgive me. My sweet Aphra, I'm falling in love with you. May I come see you today?"

Joy as life's work, joy as nourishment, joy as breath. If only for that moment, it was hers to imbibe. And she wanted to hold on. Hold on for dear life, for a dearer life than she'd known before.

In seconds, she'd dashed off a reply to Isaac that said, simply, "You can't come over soon enough for me. I've been falling in love with you for twenty years."

She dialed his cell phone number and waited, waited, waited. Each second she waited chilled her fingers by degrees, but blessed renewal was hers when she heard his phone being answered.

"Yes?" She recognized Hieu's voice.

"Hi, Hieu. It's Aphra Porter. Is Isaac around?"

"Why, hello. Snake is in his shop, working on one of his projects. He's hoping for your call. I'll go get him." Hieu put the phone down before she could thank him.

She waited, waited, waited some more, but this waiting was different. It was alive. It anticipated.

Then, "Aphra?" It was Isaac, sounding winded.

"Yes, it's me. I just got back from church and got your e-mail. Yes, please come over. Any time you want."

She'd always questioned the lucidity of those who claimed you could hear a smile on the phone. Not anymore.

"Church?" Isaac said. "I didn't know you went to church."

"I don't, not much. But Di invited me this morning, so I went."

"I've been out in the shop, rebuilding an old Mauser."

"Mouser? You're helping out an old cat?"

"Mauser." He emphasized the sibilant, a "z" sound, not an "s." "An old military rifle. This one's a late forties Israeli model."

"Okay, whatever you say. Just come over."

Aphra rejoined Di and Company, who were still on her doorstep. "You guys could have come in," she said, though now, she was glad they hadn't.

"I know, but we're enjoying this sunshine." Di studied her. "Good Lord, you look like the Lottery Grand Prize Winner Poster Child. And you haven't changed to go to the cookout. What's gotten into you?"

"I'm sorry, but may I take a rain check?"

"Don't give me that drivel. It's not raining. That's why we're having a cookout."

"Smart ass."

"Look which pot is calling which kettle black." Di wrinkled her nose at her. "Seriously, it's okay if you've changed your mind, but what's up? Something's happened. I can tell."

Aphra opened her mouth and it all fell out. "Yesterday, after Isaac looked over his Web site, we took a motorcycle ride together. Last night, when we said goodbye, he kissed me. This morning, I was worried I might never hear from him again, but just now I found out he wants to come over. Am I clear as mud?"

Tony's gaze plummeted to the toes of his sneakers. A basset hound on the brink of suicide couldn't have looked more dejected. Aphra was sorry he was hurt, but what could she do? He authored his own expectations. She never willfully added chapters.

"What are you talking about?" Di exclaimed. "Isaac Lightfoot kissed you? Hasn't he been married for, oh, at least a hundred years? If he kissed you, why did you think you wouldn't hear from him again? Why would he … How did you two wind up …" Her words couldn't match pace with her thoughts, so she gave up. "You're blowing my mind out of the water."

"He's divorced. His ex-wife is a pill, though. I met her yesterday, at his cabin. I met his son, too. And please, don't say anything about this to Mom or Bodhi. It should be me who talks to them. If it turns out there's anything to talk about."

"You met his … Oh, my God." Di exuded a long, slow breath. "All right, you owe me a long girlie talk the next time you get the chance. And don't worry, I won't run my mouth. Mum will be the word."

Aphra smiled. "Thank you."

"Please be careful, Alf. Don't get hurt, okay?"

"Don't worry, Isaac isn't an ax murderer."

Di looked at her sternly. "You know what I mean. Crushes and fantasy are one thing, but reality's a different animal. And facts are facts. Isaac Lightfoot is close to our father's age, and he has enough baggage to fill up the hold of a cruise ship."

"Not quite that much."

"If his ex-wife is hanging around him, then he certainly does."

Hardly what Aphra had wanted to hear, though she didn't say so.

8. Spider Monkey

Around mid-afternoon, Aphra's doorbell rang. She opened the front door, Isaac's name on her lips, but it wasn't Isaac who was standing there. It was the Earth Mother.

When Aphra was small, she thought her mother had eyes in the back of her head. Aphra would be climbing like a spider monkey up to the kitchen counter, ninja-silent, seeking the package of chocolate bars she knew was stashed behind the Tupperware bowls in the cabinet. As she'd reach into the shadowy depths, her questing fingertips surely mere inches from her prize, she'd hear, from the family room, the Earth Mother's stern admonishment as she sat with her back to Aphra, reading one of the books in Tolkien's trilogy *The Lord of the Rings* for the umpteenth time: "Aphrodite Rhea. Off the counter. Now."

Though she no longer believed in Anterior Extra-Ocular Organs of the Maternal Kind, Aphra was foolish to underestimate the potency of Mother Intuition.

"Honey, is everything okay?"

Aphra joined the Earth Mother outside. "Mom, you didn't have to drive over here to ask me that. I'm fine."

"It's only five miles."

"Yeah, but the traffic sucks rocks."

In a red blouse, faded blue jeans with plaid patches on the knees and rainbow-colored love beads knotted around her neck, Mom managed to look both buoyant and serious. "I got a weird feeling from Di when she told me you aren't coming to the cookout. I couldn't get anything out of her, though, so I wanted to come see you. For just a minute."

"Well, I don't know what Di led you to believe, but as you can see, I haven't sprouted a tail or a third arm. Nor have I succumbed to spontaneous human decapitation."

"Goodness knows, I'm glad you're physiologically sound. And you look lovely. But what does Di know that I don't?"

Should Aphra tell the Earth Mother? Should she not tell the Earth Mother? She had to tell her something; she might as well serve her the truth. Or at least a slice of it. But Mother Intuition outflanked her again.

"Is something going on between you and Isaac Lightfoot?"

"We've become friends. And hey, if you stick around, you can meet him, because he's coming over any minute."

She arched her eyebrow. "Isn't he around your father's age?"

Daddy was fifty-eight. "Isaac is fifty-three," Aphra admitted.

"He has a grown son. He won't want more kids. What if you want children of your own someday?"

"Good grief, Mom. Aren't you getting hasty? I said we're friends."

"Now, Alf." With those two syllables, the Earth Mother cracked open Aphra's adult husk to reveal the little girl within who was still perched on speckled white Formica, slipping a stealthy hand into the upper kitchen cabinet.

Aphra sighed. "Even when I was a kid, I didn't like being around other kids. What makes you think that raising them would be on my list of priorities?"

"I didn't come to fight. I just—"

"You just, what?"

"I just wanted to know what's going on. There's no need to get belligerent."

"Well, now you know. What there is to know, anyway. There isn't much because Isaac and I—"

Aphra was interrupted by the throaty sound of a V8 engine accentuated by a dual exhaust. She and the Earth Mother walked around to the parking lot in time to see Isaac pull his Scrambler in between Aphra's Scarab and Mom's white Toyota Camry. He got out and headed their way. As he walked, his blue jeans were snug around his sturdy thighs, and the snake skin boot on his right foot made slightly more noise on the pavement than the one on his left. The afternoon sunshine set up a glare on the lenses of his glasses. Aphra had difficulty seeing his eyes until he was standing in front of her and the Earth Mother, the brim of his brown Outback hat providing shade from the sun's rays. His big shoulders were squared beneath his khaki shirt.

Aphra's breath came faster, and she tried to speak calmly. "Isaac, I'd like you to meet my mom, Barbara. Mom, this is Isaac Lightfoot. I know you know who he is. But here he is, in three dimensions."

"Hello, Mr. Lightfoot." The Earth Mother gazed up at Isaac as though she'd been hypnotized. "If I didn't know who you were by now, though, I'd have to be blind and deaf. Alf has been reading your books since she was a kid. And talking about them. Constantly. Ever since."

Aphra rolled her eyes, but Isaac chuckled. "Please call me Isaac. And your daughter here is something else. She runs rings around those so-called Web site designers who work for my publisher."

"I'll grant you, she does very spiffy work," Mom agreed.

For a lengthy moment, the three of them stood without speaking. Then the Earth Mother hauled her gaze away from Isaac and looked at her watch. "Well, I need to get back to the cookout before Trevor turns my hamburger into a cinder. He shows no mercy to dawdlers."

"His passive-aggressive tendencies, no doubt. I guess Bodhi's there, too?"

"He can't make it. He has a meeting this afternoon—you know, one of those informal faculty pow-wows. It's probably a good thing, though. Your father is preparing for that senior level Special Topics course that's coming up this summer, and all he does is babble about Heidegger and Husserl. It makes my head hurt."

"Heidegger and Husserl would make anyone's head hurt," Aphra said. "But you know you love it. You married him for it."

"I admit it. I'm a twisted woman."

Aphra glanced at Isaac. He was smiling as he listened.

"But really, I'm dying for light conversation," Mom said. "Baseball scores. Baby names. That sort of thing. And speaking of baby names, you ought to hear some of the suggestions Tony's been coming up with. He's every bit as excited about that baby as Di and Trevor are. I was so glad to hear you went to church with them this morning."

"Yeah, well." What else was there to say? Who cared? Not Aphra. She'd rather listen to Mom discuss her spleen than Tony's damnable baby rabies. Aphra figured Tony loved babies because they reminded him of the days when his mother was wiping his ass. And if Isaac weren't there and she weren't on her best behavior, she'd tell Mom she thought so.

Oh, my. Aphra was feeling ten years old again. And Isaac looked uncomfortable.

"Well, I'm gone." The Earth Mother dug her keys out of her jeans pocket. "It was a pleasure meeting you, Isaac. I'll have to read one of your books sometime."

"Goodbye, Barbara. I enjoyed meeting you, too."

"I hope I haven't been too much of a third wheel."

"Not at all," Isaac said.

"It's just that there are times when a parent wants to make sure everything's okay." Mom flashed him a dazzling smile. "Alf will understand when she has kids of her own, won't she?"

"I guess." Inside Isaac's blue eyes began a frigid drizzle.

Aphra would love to offer her customary protestations—she fought a constant battle to keep Mom's delusions under control —but should she, in Isaac's presence, drive home the depth of her wish to avoid parenthood like hemorrhagic fever? After all, he was a father. The last thing Aphra wanted was for him to compare her unfavorably with Norma. She wasn't just his ex-wife. She was the mother of his child.

Sacred Madonna Norma versus Barren Spinster Aphra.

No, that wouldn't do.

Aphra pasted a smile on her face. "Bye, Mom. Have fun at the cookout."

"Call me soon." She got into her Camry and started its engine.

Isaac and Aphra went inside, then he took off his hat and handed it to her. She hung it on her coat rack.

"I'm sorry if Mom hurt your feelings. If it helps, I could tell she thinks you're nice. Try not to pay her any mind. She's only doing her Momma Bear thing."

His gaze clamped onto hers like a vise, then he nodded. Pilar dashed from the hall toward him and threw herself upon his boots to wallow around in feline ecstasy.

"Your notebook has become her favorite cat spot," Aphra said. "She naps on it every day."

"That cat's something else." As Isaac made his way toward the loveseat, Pilar pursued his boots. Carefully, so as not to step on her, he took a seat, and Aphra sat beside him.

Close, but not too close.

Why oh why, given that they were falling in love, were they both faltering so?

9. Behind the Blurbs

"My eyes about popped out of my head when I got out of my Scrambler and saw you all dressed up like that," Isaac said.

"Why, thank you."

"But you're gorgeous in your suede jacket, jeans, and boots, too."

"You're the only one who thinks so. Di says I seldom look like a girl."

"Well, she's wrong. And it's kind of a shame, you knocking yourself out to dress up for that Tony. From what you've said, he's kind of a sissy, isn't he?"

Aphra smothered a big, loopy grin that wanted to emerge. Sissy, did he say? Isaac was jealous! "I didn't dress up for Tony. Di and Trevor asked me to go to church, and it didn't occur to me that Tony would tag along. My mind was so full of you, I couldn't think straight. In a weird way, I was dressing up for you."

"My mind's been full of you, too." Lines of tension in his face eased. "What did your mother call you, anyway? Ralph?"

"Alf."

"Oh, I see. I always wondered what happened to you after your television show was canceled." He winked at her and leaned back in the loveseat, and Pilar snoozed on his boots.

His large boots matched his powerful build, but Aphra's feet clad in size five pumps resting next to them presented a comical portrait. Yes, a degree of sexual dimorphism was normal with adult humans, but come on—this was ridiculous.

"Pilar isn't the only girl here who likes your boots," Aphra told Isaac. "They're python skin, aren't they? I bet King Leonidas doesn't like them much." He chuckled, and she continued: "And they're huge. By comparison, I have sorry excuses for feet."

"No, you don't. You've got beautiful little feet. Like a kitten's paws."

The heated tenderness in his eyes made Aphra blush. "And look," she said. "It would take both my feet to equal one of yours."

"Well then, I reckon that makes us about equal in the foot department."

"Come again?" He'd lost her.

"My name, Lightfoot, suits me way better than my Daddy could have dreamed. I've only got one foot."

His legs terminated in two boots that, presumably, covered feet. What was he talking about?

"My left foot isn't a foot."

Oh.

"You want to see?"

"Sure."

He moved Pilar to one side, then he pulled off his boot and his sock to reveal a flesh-colored, molded-plastic approximation of a lower leg. When he pushed up the hem of his jeans, Aphra saw that his flesh-and-blood leg ended two inches below his knee. On his stump was a silicone sleeve that fit into a socket at the top of his prosthesis. The socket and the sleeve interlocked like three-dimensional puzzle pieces by means of a metal pin that protruded from the end of the sleeve. And there was a button below his knee.

"What does the button do?" Aphra asked, though she thought she knew.

"Releases the prosthesis. Guess how much it weighs."

"Hmm. It looks good and sturdy, and it functions well. You hardly limp at all. I'm going to say twelve pounds."

"Nope. Five pounds. Its innards are made of titanium, not steel. I hardly know it's on, but it sure helps me get around."

"Do you wear it all the time?"

"Pretty much, though I've got a set of crutches if I need them. About the only time I take off my prosthesis is after I shower, when I sit on the side of the tub and wash it. It, and what's left of my leg." He pointed to where the stump of his leg disappeared into the silicone sleeve.

"Does the surface of the prosthesis feel much like skin?"

"See for yourself, if you want."

Aphra did. It was smooth, like plastic, but when she applied pressure, there was some give, as there would be with a real leg.

"Polyurethane." Isaac pulled his sock, then his boot, back on. "I remember the clunky old thing I wore throughout the seventies, and much of the eighties, too. Wasn't much more than a peg leg. Prostheses are a lot better these days."

"I assume this is one of the wounds you got in Vietnam?"

"Yeah. It happened on a mission during my third tour. I was going on twenty-one years old."

"What happened?"

"My team and I were crossing a rice paddy that turned out to be booby-trapped with Punji stakes. I guess you know about Punji stakes from reading my books."

"Yes," Aphra said. "They're bamboo sticks, dipped in animal feces, that are hidden away for unsuspecting soldiers to step on."

"Well, that's a genteel way of putting it, I guess. And they didn't only use animal feces. Sometimes it was human feces. Basically, they used whatever shit they had handy. The NVA regulars and the VC hid those stakes about everywhere: in rice paddies, in jungle foliage, in pits and swamps. Anyhow, my team and I came under fire when we were crossing that paddy. The NVA were concealed behind a tree line nearby. It was an ambush. In the confusion, I wound up stepping on a stake. It went right through my jungle boot and set up gangrene in my foot that spread up my leg, and my leg had to be removed below the knee. The NVA also shot me full of 7.62 x 39 holes. I'm lucky I'm not singing *Holy, Holy* in a heavenly choir. That was my last mission, the one that got me a medical discharge."

It also got him the Silver Star for heroism. But that was all Aphra knew. She was curious about the particulars of the incident, but she wouldn't pry further. She didn't want to embarrass him.

She decided to pry about something else. "What sort of unpleasantness came up last night and kept you from writing me? Do you want to talk about it?"

"Well, I guess I'd better. When I got back home last night, the ex-wife, Norma, was waiting on me outside. She'd picked up on how you and I are feeling about each other. She started talking at me and wouldn't stop. Notice I said talking at me, not talking to me. That's what she does, she talks at people. She went on and on, and by the time I got rid of her, it was almost two o'clock in the morning, and I was worn out. I went inside, sat at my desk, and thought about writing you an e-mail, and the next thing I knew I was opening my eyes and the clock said it was almost ten o'clock in the morning. I'd fallen asleep in my chair. I felt awful about what I'd done. The last thing I wanted was for you to think I'd forgotten about you."

"She stayed until two o'clock in the morning?"

"Yeah."

"Talking to you about me?"

"Yeah."

"Why is it any of her business?" Aphra asked.

"It's none of her business, and that's what I kept telling her. But Norma's competitive. She cares only about appearances. You're a kind and caring person, Aphra, and she could tell that much on meeting you. She was never any kind of wife to me when we were married, but now that we're divorced, she can't stand the idea that I'd find somebody who's good to me and make her look bad by comparison."

"What did Norma say about me?" The words came out of Aphra's mouth even as she was asking herself, do I really want to know?

"I think you can imagine. She kept on about me being older than you. She's got me thirty years older than you, not twenty. She insists you can't be a day over twenty-three. And she kept bringing Sam into it, saying he's all upset and that he'd begged her to talk sense into me. I don't believe that, though, and even if it were true, Sam doesn't make the decisions for my life. I do."

"Twenty-three? Talk about a backhanded compliment." Aphra tightened her arms across her chest. "So what did Hieu do while all this was going on? At what was, for him anyway, an ungodly hour?"

"He slept. I talked to Norma outside. While she was talking, I wanted to just go inside and shut the door on her, but I knew she'd bang and holler and wake Hieu up. That was the kind of mood she was in. I've seen it before."

Aphra felt better, knowing Norma hadn't been in his cabin last night. She relaxed her arms. "I've got to be honest. I'm uncomfortable with the Norma thing. It doesn't bother me that you have an ex-wife, and it doesn't bother me that you have a grown son. But it bothers me that you have an ex-wife who, for whatever reason, isn't as enthusiastic about being divorced as you are. If she wants you back, then I need to step out of the way."

Isaac glanced at her in alarm. "Why the hell should you do that? Can't you tell I don't like the woman? I won't even call her 'my' ex-wife. She isn't 'my' anything."

"But you share a family with her. History."

He shook his head. "Not all histories are good. Sam's family to me, sure, but Norma? No. She's irrelevant."

"Well, what about her idyllic vision of your grandchild, yours and hers, playing under your desk at a future book signing, with the two of you looking adoringly on? Isn't there some tiny part of you that wants to share that with her?"

A scowl contorted his face. "Now, that's a crock of happy horse shit. Norma always resented my book signings. Out of all the signings I had when we were married, she went to only two and hated every second of them. She was telling the truth about having Sam with us in Atlanta that time, and he was playing under my desk and running underfoot. When I asked her to take him back to the hotel, she said no because she wanted to get under my skin. Passive-aggressive garbage, nothing more, nothing less."

"Where does Norma live?"

"In the house we lived in when we were married, in Karns Community. About fifteen minutes away from my cabin."

Aphra was familiar with Karns. Her parents' house, though it was within the city limits of Knoxville, was in the Knox County school district, and she'd attended Karns High School.

Isaac continued: "From the time Sam was born, though, I didn't live in that house with her. I lived in a storage shed in the back yard."

"You lived in a storage shed for twenty years?" Aphra asked.

"Well, I built it myself and fixed it up really nice. Had plumbing and electricity and my own refrigerator. I didn't have much space, but I got by. I slept out there, ate out there, wrote out there, and did shop projects out there. I got drunk out there, too."

"Got drunk?"

"Aphra, honey, I was a miserable human being for many years. Some of us Vietnam vets who'd seen combat had a hard time readjusting to civilian life. When I received the Silver Star, the local newspaper did a write-up on me, and that was when Norma got interested. I'd known her in high school, but we never paid much attention to each other. But after that write-up, she started coming around and flattering the stuffing out of me. Today, I can see Norma's flattery for what it was, but as a young man who was feeling less than whole, I responded to her flattery, and we wound up getting married. After my experiences in 'Nam, I thought I should want something normal. It didn't take long for me to realize I'd married somebody who was all about appearances and not much more. But as beat up as I felt, I didn't think I could do any better.

"I was disappointed that an Army career hadn't panned out for me, and I was tired of being a mechanic. I thought I might go to school over at the university and study archeology or anthropology. But I never did. Depression had sunk its teeth into me. I missed my friends from the war, the ones who had died, and the ones who were still living. John and Greg. And Hieu, who you know. The anxiety was there all the time. So I started writing, to try and deal with everything I was feeling and to speak not only for myself but for my brothers who were gone and couldn't speak anymore. Best I could, anyhow. And I started sending my stuff out. I got bunches of rejection letters at first, but I kept at it. The writing helped, and the whiskey helped some more. When I got up, I'd write for a while, and later on, I'd do my garage stuff, and on through the night, I'd drink until I fell into the bed.

"I'd never wanted children, especially not after 'Nam. Norma knew that when we married and said she accepted it, but everything changed after my first book was published. All of a sudden, she had to have a baby. She kept at me and kept at me about it, offering me her all-too-easily withheld affections, such as they were. I gave in, and Sam came into the world. One month after Sam was born, I got my ass to the doctor and had a vasectomy. I had more books in me to write, but I was damned if I was going to have so much as one more of them accompanied by a brand new, squalling baby.

"So there I was, married to a woman I didn't even like, with a sad, sweet little son depending on me. By day, I tried to buck up and do what I had to do for the people around me, and by night, after they went to bed, I was drinking myself into oblivion because I didn't like the shape of what my life had become. The NVA I could deal with, Charlie I could deal with, but against my empty day-to-day life, I was helpless, useless, disarmed. There I was, with my medals, my commendations, and my survivor's guilt, thinking about the people who died in that war, Americans and Vietnamese, so much agony, young and old people alike getting wasted, and wondering why did my friends die so I could have this? I'm telling you, Aphra, I was going down.

"But that was right around the time I got your letter, the one you sent me when you were a teenager. Something about it helped me to see myself the way you saw me. I never thought anybody but veterans like me enjoyed my books. They lived in the same world I lived in, a lot of them had the same kind of pain. But you, an intelligent, idealistic young woman, up and coming in the world, wanting to think, wanting to learn, helped me to see that maybe there might be something better in me, something good that I couldn't see. Something worth saving.

"I didn't stop drinking right then, but your letter planted a seed. As the years passed, I drank less, not more, until lo and behold, sometime around the early nineties, I didn't want so much as a drop of booze. I haven't touched the stuff in over ten years now. And I want you to know, too, that I still have your letter."

Aphra didn't know when, during Isaac's tale, the tears crept into her eyes. Nor did she know when they commenced their trek down her cheeks. She didn't make a sound, but she folded Isaac's hand in hers. Pilar reclined on Isaac's boots, and Santiago sat in front of the loveseat and took a bath.

"Even after I stopped drinking, I stayed in that storage shed until about four years ago. Then I realized I'd had enough. I was sick to death of keeping myself in storage, and I didn't want to be married to Norma Kay Ellis anymore. Now I'd broached the idea of divorce with Norma in the past, but she was always full of threats, and I'd give up divorce as not worth the pain and aggravation. She hung onto the legalities of our marriage for my money, which is downright perverse since she never read a word of my books. She became really intolerable, though, when her mother passed on. Her family had money, and she wound up with a right healthy inheritance which she lives on to this day. She opened a separate checking account and swore I'd never lay a hand on a penny of her money. As if I gave a damn about her money. The only thing I cared about was at last, when I asked for a divorce, I got it with a minimum of fuss."

Or so he thought. Melancholy washed over Aphra.

"I don't know why it took me so long to fight for what I really wanted out of life," Isaac said. "Battle fatigue, maybe. I don't know. Maybe there's something that works its way into a man's mind when he's spent so much time fighting to take, say, a hill, only to have the enemy take it right back the next day. 'Don't mean nothin'' – that's what we used to say. Right there's the definition of pointlessness, and I guess it seeped into my soul. I didn't bring much of the Warrior home with me except for the part I turned against myself. But when a man's pushing fifty, he realizes that he won't be living forever and that if he isn't at least working on getting his life close to the way he wants it, he's never going to have anything that means anything. And there you have it, the real Isaac Lightfoot, the man behind the books, the man behind the blurbs, the man behind the bullshit."

A subliminal awareness blossomed to fruition. "Isaac, I've never gotten a sense from your novels that you've experienced deep love for a woman," Aphra said. "Love between comrades in arms, yes. Love between parent and child, yes. But your treatment of romantic love makes me think it's something you've imagined more than something you've experienced."

Isaac was silent for a moment, but when he spoke, his tone was soft and measured. "I haven't said much to you yet about the new novel I've begun outlining, but it's about a soldier who's never been in love. He's lived a lot of life, gone through a lot of motions, been screwed and tattooed, but he's never been in love. And in the novel, he falls in love, for the first time in his life, with a sweet, wise young woman who pulls off his cracked and yellowed lens, who makes him see, makes him feel, makes him care about himself and about life again."

"And does this novel come from life or from imagination?" Aphra stroked his jaw, relishing his beard's coarse bristle against her hand.

"From life, Kitten." He ran his fingers through her hair, bunched it in his hands, and rubbed it across his face. He sniffed it. Tasted it. "From life."

Gently he moved Pilar off his boots. And in a twinkling, he

lifted Aphra onto his lap and overwhelmed her with his kiss.

10. Crow Feathers

And oh, that kiss. It was on the far side of the Richter Scale from the first one they shared. While their first kiss was tentative, in this one they sought to fuse their very selves together with one inexhaustible embrace. Isaac Lightfoot's kiss was everything Aphra had imagined over twenty years of dreaming and so much more, for the giver of those voracious kisses was no mere phantasm but a three-dimensional human being with all the sensory delights appertaining: the tickle of his mustache on her mouth, the warmth of his hand cradling the back of her head as he held her, the solidity of his shoulders as she clung to him like a drowning woman. Never could she have fathomed such ardor in Isaac Lightfoot for her, though his need was no more acute than hers. They were, each of them, famished for the other.

This, Aphra realized, was what was missing from her lackluster, prior liaisons: this need, licking along the surfaces of her bones like thick liquid being heated. She wanted to shroud him as the velvety blanket of night does the stars while he lit her up from within.

She wanted to make him forget Norma existed.

A mighty storm brewed, not frightening but glorious, and their mounting passion was its lightening. Within the storm's fierce gale, they'd meet and they'd revel, anointed by its drenching waters as they were swept into what would be a lush, new world for them both.

Isaac, my Isaac. Did she say it out loud? She must have because he murmured against her lips, "Yes, I'm yours" before he recommenced their kiss. Crackles of lightening heightened their mutual amplitude as rain clouds massed. The clouds couldn't contain the force of their impending deluge.

He pulled her zipper halfway down then he let it go, lifted Aphra, and carried her to her bedroom as though she weighed no more than the first raindrop that fell. Another drop fell. And another and another, syncopated with their falling raiment, and once they were in bed together unclothed, the restorative downpour broke.

Lips, hands, and fingers left neither hill nor valley uncanvassed. They were insatiable. On discovering the ropes of scar tissue that punctuated Isaac's chest, his back, his pelvic region, stomach, and both his thighs, Aphra exalted with her caresses the sites of traumas past. As she had for eighteen years, she honored his grit, and she honored his courage. She honored his sacrifices and his indomitable heart. She needed no words to tell him these things. Her touch said more than words could ever do even as his touch told her that he needed her, he had needed her all his life, she was the harmony in human life he hoped he'd someday find.

The rain fell in sheets. Their rhythm mimicked the water that nourished them as it swelled, filling them, saturating them, demanding of them more and more. As he went harder at her, went deeper into her, she clenched her eyes shut and loosed a moan against which she tasted the salty perspiration on his chest; as she raised her hips higher to meet him, forcing him further inside her, thunderclaps seized her with their power and made her cry out; and when he thrust himself into her, so deep and so hard that she felt as though she was becoming him and he was becoming her, they were tossed by rolling thunderclaps that drowned out both their voices and were violent enough to tear them into undifferentiated shreds and shards but somehow they were made whole—no, better than whole, they were one.

Aphra trembled with the aftershocks of the storm and clutched his big shoulders as he lay over her; his soft kisses rained onto her sweat-slicked forehead and her cheeks, her lips, her eyelids, and her hair: a gentle shower on their fresh, green landscape. Together, they'd created a world.

And someone was nibbling on her toes. Aphra glanced toward the foot of the bed and saw orange fluff. Pilar. She might have known. Her feet were ticklish, and barely she restrained a giggle.

"Oh please," Isaac said between kisses. Still deep inside Aphra, he was oblivious to the bed's third occupant. "Please don't ever break my heart."

He'd said, in its essence, what she wanted to say to him. "I won't.

I couldn't, not ever. To break your heart would be to break my own. I love you, Isaac. I love you."

At that, he nuzzled her cheek with his, and she felt tears there. "I'm head-over-heels, desperately in love with you," he said. "I'm a goner, honey, plain and simple, and I don't know what to do."

"What do you mean? You don't have to do anything. Just love me." Pilar's nibbles began again.

"Oh, I intend to. Love you, that is. I reckon I'm just blown away. I never thought people could feel like this. I've always thought romantic love was nothing but a crock, a bunch of silly, sentimental mush. Guess my mouth's full of crow feathers now, huh?"

"Well, if yours is, then mine is, too, as much as we've been kissing." Aphra erupted in giggles. "And I'm sorry about all this laughing. It's Pilar's fault. She's nibbling on my toes."

He chuckled. "Well, let her nibble on my toes for a while because I need to get you all cozy. Otherwise I'll squish you flat as a pancake." He rolled over and took Aphra gently along so that she wound up on top of him with her head pillowed on his burly chest. He spread her long hair out over his face then he stroked her back. Out of her peripheral vision, she detected Pilar settling herself on Isaac's feet. She was home, but she'd never felt more at home. And she'd never felt more loved. If she were a cat, she'd be purring right along with Pilar.

After their strenuous lovemaking, Aphra was possessed by languor, and buoyed by Isaac's touch, she drifted into shimmering nothingness.

Nothingness, except for the shimmering numbers on her digital clock, which read four minutes after nine o'clock. That was all she saw except for shadows. It had got dark, the window shade had been drawn, and she lay alone in bed, curled on her side. Her skin was cool and dry, and the covers were tangled. She'd been asleep for over three hours. Where had Isaac gone?

One shadow separated itself from the rest of them and crabbed across the doorway of her bedroom. It was too big to be Pilar or Santiago. But if it was Isaac, he didn't make a sound.

Aphra reached for the lamp on her nightstand and flipped it on. Isaac's eyeglasses were gone, and his clothes and boots were gone from the floor. Was he sneaking out? Had his ex-wife called him on his cell phone, making him regret what he'd shared with Aphra? If only she could get the cotton out of her head—she couldn't think. Why should waking from a nap be more difficult than waking from regular sleep?

If that was Isaac she'd seen in the doorway, he'd either shrunk or was moving in a crouch. Could he have discovered someone trying to break in?

She went into the bathroom adjoining her bedroom, found her robe, and pulled it on. Maybe no one was breaking in and Isaac wasn't pining for his ex. Maybe he was in the kitchen making a sandwich, as well he should, for all evening food had been forgotten, the demand of their growling stomachs secondary to the call of their conversation, and later, that of their passion.

She didn't have to go far to find Isaac. Six feet from her bedroom doorway he appeared, looming over her. She didn't hear him coming, nor did she see him, until he was there. She had a quick glimpse of his face in the light that spilled over from her bedroom —stony eyes, an unrelenting jaw—before he had her in a headlock; her back was to him, and she didn't remember him turning her around. He was fast, big, and strong. And he could break her neck like a twig.

She let out a squeak; it was all she could manage. He abruptly spun her back around and pressed her up against him. "My God, it's you. You startled me. Oh, please forgive me. What a sorry-assed son of a bitch I am!"

Aphra was thankful she hadn't needed to use the bathroom, or else she'd be shucking off her robe and throwing it into the washing machine. But she was shaking.

He held her tighter. "Look at you, I've scared you half to death. Did I hurt you, honey? God almighty, I'm sorry. I woke up crazy-headed, plumb off my rocker."

She hugged him back and nuzzled his chest. The rough hair there grazed her face; he hadn't buttoned his shirt. "It's okay, sweetheart. You haven't hurt me. What do you mean, crazy-headed? Is someone trying to break in?"

"Nobody except for old ghosts," Isaac said.

"Do you mean you had a nightmare?"

"Not a nightmare, at least not one I remember. All I know is I woke up in a cold sweat, terror freezing my bones. I felt like something awful was going to happen, and there you were, my sweet little kitten, lying on top of me. I had to make sure you were safe. So there I was, putting on my clothes then humping around this place, looking for potential ambush sites and figuring out the best defensive positions against them. I don't know what got into me, but I know it hasn't gotten into me for a long time."

"Are you saying you do this often? Wake up and go into battle mode?"

"It used to happen pretty regularly. Not anymore. Mostly when it happens these days, it's triggered by stress."

"I'm stressing you out?"

"No, it isn't you. Well, not really. Not your sweet self. I already feel so easy with you. It's more the situation. I guess that forming a connection with you, growing to love you not only as a woman but as a friend, reminds me of the last time I formed deep connections. With my friends in 'Nam. I loved those guys, and so many of them died."

Aphra thought she understood. "Come into the kitchen with me. I'll fix us a pot of coffee and something to eat. And maybe it would do you good to talk. I think you have a lot inside that you haven't shared with anyone except your friends from the war, and if you want to share with me, then I want to listen."

He hugged her again. "Now, that's the best idea I've heard in many months of Sundays."

11. Alpha Bravo

Aphra rooted through her kitchen provisions, in search of ingredients. In her cabinets, there was spaghetti and marinara sauce; in her refrigerator, there was ground beef, sour cream, and three kinds of cheese: ricotta, mozzarella, and cheddar. A vision presented itself to Aphra's mind, and when she shared it with Isaac, he responded enthusiastically. He sat at her kitchen table, his gaze fond as he watched her cooking spaghetti, browning beef, simmering sauce, and grating cheeses and mixing them with the sour cream before layering it all together in a casserole dish to comprise their feast.

She put her culinary opus in the oven to bake then sat at the table beside Isaac. "It'll be ready in forty-five minutes."

"Plenty of time to talk, then." He frowned. "I feel rotten about flaking out on you the way I did."

"It's all right." She covered his hand with hers. "Please, tell me anything about Vietnam that you're comfortable telling me. Go easy on yourself."

"Well, going easy isn't easy for me, if you get my meaning. I revert to battle mode when a helicopter flies overhead. It isn't obvious to people who don't know me well, but when I hear the sound of a chopper, I stiffen up and my mind goes back in time some thirty-odd years. I feel myself gripping the handset of that PRC-25, the radio we used. And look here at how I'm sitting at this table with my back against the wall, looking out towards your front door. I never sit facing away from routes of ingress or egress or with my back to crowds of people. It's something that hasn't left me, and I don't think it ever will. You sure you want to fool with a crazy guy like me?"

"Yes, I'm sure," Aphra said. "More sure than I've ever been about anything. And you're not crazy. You've been through a whole hell of a lot. More than most people could conceive of."

"Most people, yeah, but not all," he said and sighed. "I guess I should start with my last mission, the one where I lost my foot. You've probably figured out it's the mission they gave me the Silver Star for and one of my Purple Hearts. As I said before, it was an ambush. Alpha Bravo. Several of my brothers were killed that day, but Hieu survived, and so did John and Greg. All three were badly wounded. I saved their lives and I'm glad about that, but I couldn't save Buck, Andy, and the others. I moved them to cover, but they were so terribly wounded that they died, either right there on the spot or later, after being taken to the M.A.S.H. unit."

"So you moved your fallen comrades to cover after you were wounded yourself? After stepping on that Punji stake, after having been shot?"

"Rangers don't leave Rangers behind," Isaac said flatly. "My Silver Star citation says 'for conspicuous gallantry above and beyond the call of duty,' but it's wrong, see. Since I would have given my life for my friends, nothing I did for them was 'above' or 'beyond' the call of any 'duty.' My recon team was heavy that day, ten of us guys were out on patrol instead of just five. I keep my medal tucked in a shoe box in the closet along with pictures of my friends. That's where it belongs, with those guys."

Stroking his hand, Aphra said only, "Tell me." Isaac's fingers were cold.

"I stepped on that Punji stake when the ambush started. In all the confusion, I hardly felt it. And I wasn't the one who got it the worst from those damn stakes. Buck was a darned sight unluckier than me. He was a skinny little guy from New York City. Tough as a pine knot. He was also a brilliant jazz pianist and one of the finest soldiers I've ever known. He and Andy, his best buddy since grade school, were drafted at the same time, and they were the first friends I made after arriving in 'Nam. The day of the ambush, when the firing began, Buck dove for cover, trying to flatten himself out in that rice paddy, and he got a shit-covered stick in the gut for his trouble. While he was lying there screaming his head off, a fuck-you lizard ran onto his back and pissed on him."

"A fuck-you lizard?"

"Gecko," Isaac said. "We called 'em fuck-you lizards because of the noise they made. Sounded like they were always saying 'fuck you, fuck you.' You know, like 'fuck you, GI, go home.' Can't stand the sight of the things to this day. I look away from them when I go to the pet store to get mice for King Leonidas. Anyhow, when my brothers started falling all around me, I lost it. All that drove me was the need to give Nathaniel Victor hell for payback. They say I killed twenty NVA who, as it turned out, were the forward elements of a battalion. I used my radio to call in air support, which came in later to pretty much smoke all their asses. Later, as in too late for my brothers. As least the fog wasn't as bad that day as it usually was in the A Shau Valley, where most of our missions were conducted, so the fighter bombers could do their thing.

"In the meantime, all I knew was that I opened up on those little guys in black pajamas, both where I could see 'em and where I couldn't. I could figure out their positions from how they were hitting the guys on my team. And just like it was with my foot, I hardly felt anything, even when they shot me all to hell. I just kept on going, blowing away as many NVA as I could and dragging my wounded and dying friends into the tree line for cover, until finally I fell on my knees at the medic's feet with Hieu on my shoulders, our blood all mixed together and my smoking CAR-15 in my hand. The medic took Hieu from me, and that's when I passed out. I was told later that the medic had needed to pry my rifle from my fingers. I was evac'd to a M.A.S.H. unit where I had several emergency surgeries. But I don't remember a thing until a week later, when I woke up in a German military hospital."

Aphra shivered, squeezed his hand. "What was the extent of your injuries?"

"For starters, I almost bled to death. And in addition to losing my foot and part of my leg to gangrene, I had a lacerated liver, a collapsed lung, peritonitis from the gunshot wounds to my gut, a fractured pelvis, and a broken right femur. It was a long time before I could walk again, and it was an even longer time before I could walk without crutches. After I was stabilized, I was given a ticket back to the World: Walter Reed Army Medical Center in Washington, D.C. And then as I was being wheeled off the plane, I got a face full of shit, thrown by a protester who'd been hiding behind the fence. God knew I'd had enough shit in my foot, and then I was damned if I didn't get it in the face, too."

"Oh, no." Aphra got up and put her arms around Isaac from behind. "I'm sorry. I can't imagine how that must have felt."

"Well, it sure wasn't pleasant. Especially not after growing up with Daddy's stories about how the World War II veterans were welcomed home as heroes." He paused, then said: "I stayed at Walter Reed until the end of August, then I had several months of rehab there before getting my medical discharge and making it back to Tennessee for Christmas, clunky peg leg and all. It was a really bad time. If Daddy had been around, he could have helped me. He would have understood since he'd been in combat himself, but he'd died of a massive stroke when I was still in high school. I missed him so much. And Momma, she said something in my eyes was scaring her half to death, that I wasn't her little boy anymore. She had to get to know me again. I don't think the situation was any easier for her than it was for me. And my injuries screamed 'Vietnam vet.' In Solway things weren't too bad, but in Knoxville, where I sometimes went to get parts for my work at the garage, I got a fair bit of spitting and cursing from card-carrying members of the Peace and Love Contingent."

"Oh, sweetheart." Aphra didn't know what else to say, but she rubbed his shoulders gently.

"You know, Hieu does the same thing with his medals that I do. I didn't know that until he brought it up just the other week. Funny, isn't it, to find that out after all these years?" But he wasn't laughing.

Aphra returned to her chair. "Have you talked to your ex-wife..." She couldn't bring herself to say Norma's name; perhaps she feared raising her up from the Undivorced— "about these things?"

He shook his head. "Not much. Norma wasn't a good person to talk to about the war. It made her weird in the head; well, weirder than normal, if you can dig that. Whenever the subject came up, she'd call me a killer and go on about how she was afraid of me, though initially she was attracted to what she saw as the prestige of my medals. And she was hateful to my friends. It didn't take long before Hieu, John, and Greg couldn't come around at all without a lot of grief from her. So every few years, we'd arrange two week hunting and fishing vacations out West, away from all our homes. We'd go to Montana. Idaho. Wyoming. And sometimes we'd go to DC, to visit the Wall."

"Where are John and Greg now?'

"Greg's okay. We keep in touch by phone and e-mail. Over the years, he struggled with addiction to Darvon and Demerol, but he was finally able to get clean and stay clean. He runs a construction company up in South Dakota. His mother's full-blooded Lakota Sioux, and Greg was born on the Pine Ridge Reservation. He and his wife had have their ups and downs, but they're still married. Their son, Chris, has spina bifida and he's been in a wheelchair all his life. Greg was exposed to Agent Orange in Vietnam, and he thinks that's where Chris's problems come from.

"John joined the Army to get money for college. After the war, he went to medical school and became a research doctor. He later married a war widow who had three little kids. In 'Nam we all called him Daddy-o because at twenty-seven, he was the oldest guy on our team. But John's dead now. Heart attack got him. Two years ago." Isaac's voice broke and he stared at his hands.

Aphra got up again and kissed his cheek, hoping to give him some measure of comfort. "What about Hieu? How are things with him?"

Isaac cleared his throat. "Not so good. I'm worried about him. I don't think I've told you about this, but he had a wonderful first wife. They'd been married a year or so by the time he was working with my team, so I got to meet her. She was a doll. So sweet, so good to him, and he adored her. But soon after the war ended, she died having their first child, and the child died, too. Then, less than a year later, Hieu hooked up with his second wife. A rebound thing, I guess. She was fussy and demanding. Really hateful. When she and Hieu came to America, she got worse. Hieu got a degree in computer science and landed a good job, but all he ever heard from his wife was that he wasn't making enough money. And now she's trying to take poor Hieu for everything he's got."

The kitchen timer dinged, and Aphra removed the casserole, hot and bubbly, from the oven.

"Man oh man. That looks great."

Aphra's cats joined them in the kitchen: Pilar cozied up to Isaac's boots, and Santiago sat near the table and kept a cagey eye on Isaac. Aphra and Isaac were silent as they ate, lost in their thoughts.

12. Learning to Float

When they finished their meal, Isaac seemed preoccupied.

"What's the matter?" Aphra asked. "Maybe that's a stupid question, after everything you've told me."

"No, it's not a stupid question. I do have something on my mind, and it's nothing to do with Vietnam. Talking about 'Nam has helped this old soldier a lot already. There's something else chewing on me."

"What is it? Please tell me."

"It was what your mother was talking about. About how you might want children someday. And the more I think about it, the more it's getting to me. Now I can understand her Momma Bear thing about me being so much older than you. It's parental protectiveness, which I relate to. To tell you the truth, I wasn't overly pleased when Sam married Cheryl. I thought he could have done a lot better for himself, though I've made my peace with her now. Your momma will either allow herself to get to know me, or she won't. It's her decision. But Aphra, I can't produce more children. There are no tadpoles swimming in the stream, and there haven't been for a quarter-century. Practically speaking, my vasectomy isn't reversible. And it worries me to think that, over the long haul, you might come to want something you can't get from me. Wouldn't that two-footed, fertile young man your momma likes so much be a better bet for you than I am?"

Oh, my, Aphra thought. She should have felt freer to argue with Mom in front of Isaac. "Sweetheart, ask anyone who has known me for a long time, and they'll all tell you the same thing. I don't want children. I'm not the least bit interested in spending the next twenty years performing the day-to-day activities necessary to motherhood. As you know, I'm a private person, and I need lots of quiet and personal space. The hustle and bustle of parenthood would drive me nuts. If I were a mother, I'd love my kids, but I'd be miserable, and kids deserve better than a miserable parent. I'm the odd one out with the women in my family. I want different things from life than they do. So don't worry about the Mommy Bug biting me. I'd say I'm pretty darned immune."

Isaac smiled, nodded. "I'm relieved to hear it."

In talking about his experiences in Vietnam, Isaac had shared something of his heart with Aphra, and she yearned to do the same for him. But what did she have? Though she'd fought her share of battles, she'd never been in a shooting war. She thought about the twenty short stories she deemed keep-worthy which resided in a three ring binder in her office. Since the beginning of her friendship with Isaac, she'd longed to share one of her stories with him—perish the thought, more than one!—but she'd been reluctant to do so. She wasn't sure why. Maybe she was afraid he wouldn't like the story. Maybe she was afraid he'd think her a mooch, a hanger-on who was trying to use him as a leg-up in the publishing game.

Maybe, most of all, she was afraid of presenting herself to him in her old guise: that of a groupie.

"Isaac?"

He looked at her, his gaze tender. "Yeah, Kitten?"

"Would you like a short story for dessert?"

"Actually, I had something else in mind for dessert." He slipped his hand inside her robe and squeezed her shoulder. "But a short story would be nice, too." He grinned at her. "Seriously, I'd love to read one of your stories. I was wondering if you were ever going to ask."

Wow. Isaac Lightfoot wanted to read one of her stories. The stars in her eyes might go nova. And oh my, she was slipping into fan mode again, as though she and Isaac had never met, as though he hadn't become her friend as well as her favorite author, as though they hadn't spent the evening making love to each other with an intensity of which she'd never dreamed mere mortals capable.

Oh, why not. She'd show him a story. Her desire to share was greater than her fear. Her lover could be her mentor, too. She had to remember that he was no longer "Isaac Lightfoot" to her. He was Isaac. She wasn't a groupie anymore.

"Don't go anywhere. I'll be right back." She gave him a huge smile.

From the binder in her office, she took out *Learning to Float*, the story of which she was the most proud, written two years ago. It was about a woman, young but not too young, who lived alone. Her passion was singing, but she was afraid to sing in front of an audience. The story operated on dual levels: it wove together the importance of finding one's voice with the struggle to trust enough in life's waters to float without fear of sinking, by analogy to the main character's childhood memories of learning to swim.

As a child in swim class, Ellen had braved the water and floated only after she thought she saw another child doing it first. But she was mistaken. The other child didn't float at all—his feet were touching the bottom of the pool. As things turned out, Ellen was first in her class to float and went on to become a skillful swimmer.

As an adult, after weeks of agonizing, Ellen fortified her guts to attend Karaoke Night at a local bar and grill. She witnessed all sorts of singers including, to her surprise and pleasure, a shy woman like herself who gritted her teeth and took the stage. But the woman froze like a deer in headlights at the opening chords of her song, dropped the microphone, and fled to the bathroom. Ellen cringed in sympathetic horror and couldn't bring herself to go onstage, though when she got back home, she sang, alone in her living room, the song she'd wanted to sing at the bar.

The story ended when a little boy who lived across the street, with whom Ellen was friendly and who had heard her voice through her open living-room window, came to her door to tell her how beautiful her voice was. Would you, he implored her, sing at my birthday party next weekend? Yes, she told him, I will. And maybe after the party, she'd return to Karaoke night and let 'em hear something really special.

From the time he started reading her Aphra's story, Isaac was engrossed, stroking his mustache at intervals. A smile flitted across his lips here and there, at other points he narrowed his eyes in scrutiny as though he'd needed to read something twice for clarification. Once he let roll with a belly laugh so contagious that Aphra laughed, too. She loved watching Isaac do anything. Read. Laugh. Even breathe.

When he finished her story, the expression on his face was warm and contemplative. He met her gaze and nodded in satisfaction. "Your characters come alive, and I love your sense of humor. The scene in the bar cracked me up, where Ellen is wondering if that loud-mouthed, self-ordained diva is going to electrocute herself from spraying so much spit on the microphone when she sings. And I got a kick out of your description of that diva stroking the microphone like it's, shall I say, a phallic object. You've got good work here, Kitten. Low key, but deeply felt."

She blushed at his praise. To say he'd provided her with encouragement would be to say that winning the grand prize in a lottery was a positive financial development. "Do you have any criticism, though?" she asked. "Don't worry about hurting my feelings. I believe that I'm a decent writer, but I want to get better. I want my work to be publishable, and the only way to get better is to be aware of how I might be going wrong."

He smiled at her. "Okay. One piece of advice I'll give you is this: don't try so hard to sculpt your prose. Let the words flow with the meaning of what you're trying to say, the story you're trying to tell. I can tell you have a natural ear for prose rhythms. Your style is musical, and your storytelling is engaging. But you need to trust your instincts. Don't intellectualize things into the ground—it slows down the story. Am I making sense to you?"

"I think so. Sometimes I feel bottled up when I write. It comes from my anxiety, my self-doubt. I'll take your advice to heart. But do you like the story, plot-wise?"

"Very much. I like how, in the end, Ellen gets her approving audience after all. A person might expect the story to end with Ellen brooding in her living room, thinking about how her voice will never be heard by anybody. But it doesn't end like that, and that's good. I like characters who are moved to action, not to self-pity. Your story is a testament to the element of chance in life's most intimate struggles. It illustrates the insidiousness of life patterns that operate below conscious perception. And it demonstrates the chancy nature of building confidence, the brittleness of our will to face life head-on, and how we must always keep that will fortified. Dovetails nicely with themes I deal with in my books."

Aphra was thrilled by how he'd sliced down to the core of her story. After sitting for some seconds and grinning at him like an idiot, she finally said, "Well, you've been my inspiration for years.

I've often thought that I feel as you do about many things."

"I'd say you're spot-on correct. Keep up the good work. You've impressed me mightily tonight."

Aphra wondered if she'd ever again be able to fit her head through a standard doorway. "Thanks. I'm going to send that story to a magazine tomorrow, before I lose my gumption."

"Good for you. That's exactly what you need to do."

She had a magazine in mind, too. She had for some time. It was *The Blotter*, a small literary magazine. They claimed a mercifully brief response time. But what if they didn't like *Learning to Float* as much as Isaac did? What if. Aphra could spend the rest of her life stagnating in the brambles alongside her chosen path, asking herself "What if."

But she didn't want to do that anymore.

Aphra's gaze locked affectionately with Isaac, and for a moment, she felt married to him. My, what a serendipitous thought. What did the future hold for them?

"Are you uncomfortable with our age difference?" she asked. "You know, with other people?"

He looked taken aback. "Lord, no!" he exclaimed. Did he protest too much, Aphra wondered. But he continued, somewhat more calmly, with, "It's a load of bull the way some people might be inclined to see our relationship. But we know the truth, and that's what matters."

"It's Sam you're thinking about, isn't it?"

He smiled at her wryly. "I guess so. I wish people cared more about getting to the truth of things, and yes, I admit I'm hoping Sam will be able to do that. But it's his choice whether he does or not. He's grown, so hopefully he's figured out that life doesn't have to match TV talk show mentality. If he gives you a chance, I know he'll like you."

This encouraged Aphra, and she smiled back.

"In fact, I want Momma to meet you. I'm thinking it'll do her heart good to see her favorite son with somebody who thinks he's worth more than a pinch of salt. And it'll give me a chance to show you off."

"Sounds great." In truth, however, the prospect terrified Aphra. Hadn't Norma said, in her oh-so-vainglorious tone, that she and Isaac's mother were like mother and daughter? If that were the case, then Isaac's mother might resent a young upstart appearing on her son's horizon.

Further analysis was abandoned, however, when Isaac pulled Aphra from her chair. He untied the sash of her robe, reached inside, and cupped the cheeks of her naked butt. He squeezed her there gently, then firmly.

"I'm proud of you, you know." His voice was rough with desire. "You're the sexiest, most remarkable woman I've ever known."

If she was remarkable, it was only because she was a humanoid torch. And her brain was a marshmallow, toasted by her craving for Isaac. Oh, what his touch did to her! She stroked his bristly cheek. "Then love me. Love me all over the place. Here in the kitchen, where the fires are good and hot."

"God almighty, I'd say hot! It can't be any hotter than we are." He slipped the robe from her shoulders, and her mouth was engulfed by his luscious kiss. Naked, she sagged in his arms and pulled at his jeans with liquefying fingers, imploring those jeans down, down, out of her way, because if she didn't have Isaac deep inside her within one split second, she'd experience a meltdown of staggering proportions. He obliged her, then they either lowered themselves to the kitchen floor or the floor rose to meet them, because he was on his back and she was on top of him, and his hands were filled with her breasts, holding her nearly vertical as she bounced faster and faster, harder and harder, putting on quite a show for two stupefied cats who had never witnessed such indecorous goings-on transpiring upon their virgin tile. And as the kitchen air filled with their wordless entreaties, they were back in their fresh world, their green world, theirs and theirs alone, whose rain mirrored the sweat that bathed her, whose thunder echoed the spasms that rocked her.

They went to bed, and as they neared sleep, Aphra asked, "Why does Hieu call you Snake?"

"He said I was like the poisonous snakes there. Stealthy as can be and lethal when I struck."

"Well, you don't look like a snake. You look like a bear."

"I'll tell Hieu you said so."

And when morning came and Aphra awakened, she was in the arms of her bear, and he was sleeping peacefully.

13. Nest of Snipers

Aphra was loath to get up before Isaac. She loved lying in his arms but there was something she wanted to do before he woke up. So while he slept, she found scissors and thread, a tube of glue, and a length of cord. She sat in the rocking chair beside her bedroom window, opened the shade, and lay her supplies on the sill. Bathed in morning sunshine, she used the scissors to cut a lock of her hair, out of which she fashioned a bracelet for her bear.

She'd completed her task when she heard a soft snore from the bed. Isaac flopped onto his back and opened his eyes, roused to wakefulness by Pilar's nose touching his. He stroked the cat's back, and she arched with pleasure against his hand.

"What a wake-up," he said. "You're right cute, fuzzball, but I would have preferred your momma."

Aphra went to the bedside and kissed Isaac's lips. "How's that, then?"

He was rapt as he gazed at her and they spoke at the same time:

"God, I love kissing you first thing in the morning."

"I made something for you."

Aphra lifted his hand, and around his brawny wrist she tied the bracelet. It already looked like it belonged there.

"What's this?" He moved his wrist up to his face.

"It's a bracelet. I made it out of a lock of my hair. I woke up thinking about how I want you to have something of me with you all the time."

"Thank you. This is precious." He stroked the bracelet with one finger, then his eyes grew misty and he pulled her down on the bed and held her close. "I love that beautiful hair of yours. I commented on it when we were first getting to know each other. Remember?"

"Autumn's breath burning," she said.

"Down your back," he finished.

They spent the morning in bed, making love, playing with the cats, and talking about silly things such as which cat had the longest whiskers and whose butt, Isaac's or Aphra's, was the cuter. Neither of them wanted to leave their four-poster island, but it became inevitable by noon when they could no longer ignore their growling stomachs.

They prepared pancakes together, laughing at the odd creations that took shape in Aphra's skillet. Neither Aphra nor Isaac was good at pouring batter without spatter, but the pancakes were pleasing gastronomically if not aesthetically. After breakfast, Aphra got *Learning to Float* ready to send to *The Blotter*, and Isaac called Hieu.

"Hi, buddy. I'm at Aphra's." Aphra heard a smile in Isaac's deep voice which she had no doubt Hieu would hear, too. "Oh, you did, did you? Well, well … Yes, we're having a great time. Mmm hmm. Yes, she's lovely, and yes, she's sweet … Hey now, Swampy, get your own girl. I got to go. Hold down the fort. Bye."

He turned to Aphra. "Hieu's happy for us, Kitten. And he likes you a lot."

"That's wonderful. I like Hieu, too."

"I'm glad you do."

Then Isaac called his mother. "Hi, Momma. Would you like some company this afternoon? I want you to meet somebody… Yes, it's a lady. A sweet young lady I'm crazy about… What time? Oh, in another hour or so, I reckon. All right. We'll see you then." Hanging up, he looked at Aphra and said, "She's intrigued."

"I guess that's a good sign," Aphra said, trying to sound sprightly.

Isaac studied her. "You're not nervous, are you?"

"Well, I have to admit, I am. The other day, when you were in your shop getting that welder for Sam, Norma talked to me about how close she and your mother are. I understand that since you and Norma were married for so long, but if your mother likes Norma so much, she might resent me being a part of your life. Especially if she's gotten wind that Norma doesn't like it."

"Don't worry. Momma will like you. She's nice to Norma because Norma's the mother of her grandchild. But she's seen how Norma, for all those years, treated me like something nasty she wanted to scrape off her shoe. Momma's not blind, she's not dumb, and being seventy-four, she sure as hell wasn't born yesterday."

He winked, and Aphra burst out laughing.

"And," Isaac continued, "I believe Momma cares enough about me to be happy that I'm happy."

"Thanks, Bear. That helps." And it did.

But on entering Maggie Lightfoot's tidy, white house, Aphra wanted to turn right back around and leave.

It wasn't Maggie Lightfoot Aphra found disconcerting. Maggie was a stout woman with hair like white cotton-candy, and she smelled of lilacs, a scent that emanated from her lavender-colored skirt. And she was more than gracious as she took Aphra's hand and greeted her. What Aphra found disconcerting was Maggie's living room: its walls were blanketed with family photographs, many of which exalted a definition of "family" that felt like cold water in Aphra's face, bringing her back to reality.

Some of the photos depicted Maggie with Isaac's father; those intrigued Aphra. When she first saw the black-and-white shots of Isaac's father in uniform, she thought they were of a stern-faced, clean-shaven Isaac dressed up for a World War II re-enactment. Maggie's then-youthful face was radiant as her fluffy hair grazed her husband's sturdy shoulder. And some of the pictures showed Isaac as a boy. These were even more fascinating to Aphra than the photographs of his parents. What a handsome youngster Isaac had been, the rugged angles of his boyish face and the width of his pre-adolescent shoulders suggesting the strapping, handsome man he was today.

But it was hard to take pleasure in those relics, for scattered among them were numerous photos of Norma: Isaac with Norma, Isaac with Norma and Sam, and various permutations thereof. There was Isaac and Norma's wedding picture, him in his Army uniform and her in a lacy dress, hat and gloves. Norma's hair was reddish then, not the color of bronze. Her gaze, however, was varnished with a brittle sheen that hardly fit the face of a loving, blushing bride. She leaned noticeably away from the youthful Isaac, who was still on crutches and wasn't smiling at all, not even out of his eyes.

And dominating the wall to the left of Maggie's couch was

a family portrait, two feet wide by three feet tall, presented in a decorative pewter frame, from which a mustached Isaac, a primped-up Norma, and a sailor-suited baby boy gazed out stolidly in perpetuity. That portrait was surrounded by many more photos which chronicled three generations of Lightfoots, to which Aphra was but a retrograde onlooker: there was Isaac, alone in his uniform and ponderous with medals, a wedding ring on his left hand; there was a little boy, Sam, holding a puppy, there was Maggie in a swim suit perching her dripping grandson on one knee, Norma, in a skirted suit, standing behind her holding a beach towel, and Isaac, presumably, operating the camera. It was a pictorial celebration of the Lightfoot family that marked, for the individuals who comprised it, an exclusive club. And in that club, Norma clearly remained a member in good standing.

Isaac noticed Aphra's examination of the photos. Something must have shown on her face because he studied them as though he'd never seen them before, then he let out a long breath.

"Call me Miss Maggie," Isaac's mother said to Aphra.

Aphra swallowed hard and smiled. "Thank you. And please call me Aphra."

"Aphra? What an unusual name."

"It's short for Aphrodite."

Maggie raised a sculpted eyebrow. "You must have been born during those flower child years."

"I guess it's pretty obvious, huh?"

"Well, have a seat, why don't you?" Maggie indicated her couch, and Aphra complied. "Can I get you something cool to drink? I've got plenty of pop, and I've got iced tea, too."

Aphra's mouth was dry as a desert, so she accepted Maggie's offer of tea. Isaac went to the kitchen and got a can of soda, then he sat beside Aphra. Maggie brought her a fluted glass of iced tea with a lemon wedge, then she took a seat in a brown plush recliner.

"So where are you from, Aphra?" Maggie asked.

"I've lived in Knoxville all my life. My parents have lived here a long time, too. Their names are Larry and Barbara Porter. I have a younger sister named Diana."

"The oldest child always gets it the worst, huh?" Maggie smiled at Aphra then she looked at the hair bracelet on Isaac's wrist. "What on earth's that? It looks like hair off some kind of animal."

"It's a bracelet. Aphra made it for me."

"How nice. It reminds me of how Sam used to make rings out of earthworms when he was just a little guy. I remember how he'd cry when they wouldn't stay on his fingers and kept crawling off." Maggie glanced out the window then she smiled at Aphra again. Was there an anticipatory quality to Maggie's smile? Perhaps Aphra was imagining things because she was trying not to be unnerved by Maggie's photographs. Aphra wrenched her gaze from the images on the walls and sipped her tea, which was really quite good.

"I guess you're wondering how Aphra and I met," Isaac said to his mother.

"Sure, I was just fixing to ask."

"It was at my latest book signing. Aphra happened to mention that she designs Web sites, and I got her to update mine. She got it done the other day, and it looks great. If you'd let me fix you up with a computer, Momma, you could check it out. It's slick as can be."

"I've told you, I don't want anything to do with those newfangled machines. They give me the creeps."

"If you and Aunt Peggy both had computers, you could e-mail each other every day."

"Plain ol' fashioned paper and stamps works just fine."

"Aphra doesn't just design Web sites," Isaac said. "She's a crackerjack writer, too."

"Oh?" Maggie regarded Aphra with more interest. "How many books have you got out?"

"None," she admitted. "I love to write, but I've never submitted my work. Isaac is encouraging me, though."

Maggie nodded. "Well, I sure never dreamed Isaac would become a writer. He worked as a mechanic before and after the war. He's handy, just like his daddy was. I don't know what I'd do without him. If it weren't for him, my house would be falling apart. My car, too."

"Well, I have to say I like working on that car a lot better than the one you had before. That thing about ran me crazy."

"And how far along is Cheryl, again? When is she going to make me a great-grandma?"

"Sam told me sometime around late September."

Maggie gazed out the window again, her expectant quality

peaking, and Aphra followed her gaze to a Dodge Neon that was parking in the driveway. And who should emerge from the Neon but Norma and Sam as though rendered in flesh and blood from the effigies that surrounded Aphra. As they marched in lockstep toward Maggie's door, Aphra saw through the window that Norma's eyes glittered like the gold bangles on her wrist. Clad in a purple pantsuit with a wide, black leather belt, she was decked out more for an office party than for a visit to her former mother-in-law's home. Sam, on the other hand, wore faded jeans that were covered with grease.

Isaac touched Aphra's shoulder and stood up. Following his lead, she stood, too, though she'd prefer to sink into Maggie's carpet and render herself inseparable from its blue fibers. What was the difference? She was being trod upon anyhow; she might as well make it official.

"We're going on." Isaac's voice was rougher, deeper than normal, though he didn't otherwise betray his anger.

Maggie ushered Norma and Sam inside before they could knock. "You don't have to rush off. It isn't like you've never seen these folks before."

"I expected better from you, Mom. And yes, we—" He placed special emphasis on the word *we*. "—have to go."

"Where have you been?" Norma demanded of Isaac as she stood elbow-to-elbow with Sam, who looked at Aphra like he'd never seen her before. "I kept calling you last night, but all I got was your voice mail. Running the roads late these days, huh?"

"My hours are my own to do with as I please," Isaac said. "What did you want?"

"I wanted us to do some planning." She gestured subtly toward Sam. "And I just wanted to talk."

"Yeah, we'll talk all right, but not now." Isaac took Aphra's arm. "Come on, let's go."

In Isaac's Scrambler, as he drove, Aphra knotted her hands in her lap and gazed out the passenger window. She didn't know where they were going, and she didn't care as long as the operant direction was "away." Isaac must have turned off the ringer for his cell phone while he was visiting. For that, Aphra was thankful. She was hard-pressed to imagine anything more repellent than Isaac accepting a call from Norma while he was making love to her,

Aphra.

The touch of Isaac's rough palm on her neck, under her hair, startled Aphra, and she jumped.

"I'm sorry about what happened back there," he said. "I never dreamed ..."

"It's okay."

"After I told Momma we were coming, she must have called Norma. And Norma had probably put a bug in her ear to get her to do it."

"Really, it's okay."

"No, it isn't."

They were heading down one of Solway's many narrow side roads, and Isaac pulled the Scrambler off into a grassy field then gathered Aphra up in a hug. She patted his shoulders perfunctorily then let go of him and sat back in her seat.

"Are you sure this is a good idea?" she asked.

"What?" He looked befuddled. "You mean, you want to go back to Momma's?"

"Oh shit, no. Not in a million years. I mean, you and me in general. Is this a good idea? After all, Norma wants you back. It's official. She's even conscripted your mother to help her out."

"I wouldn't care if Norma raised up Patton's Third Army from the dead and conscripted every last one of 'em. It wouldn't make any difference to me. I don't want to go back to her. Not ever. Do you remember what I told you last night, or didn't you listen to me at all?"

Aphra's tears flowed. "Of course I did."

"Oh God, don't cry." He folded her to him again and smoothed her hair. "I'm sorry, honey. I'm so sorry."

"All those pictures," Aphra sobbed. "All that history. I felt so out of place. Compared to Norma, I'm nothing to you. Nothing."

He kissed the tears from her cheeks. When her sobs quieted, he said, "My sweet Kitten, you're wrong. As I've said before, not all histories are good. There's nothing for you to compete with because Norma's not in the race. She was never anything but a source of stress and misery for me."

"She's the source of your son, isn't she?"

Isaac shrugged. "That big Super Center store they plunked down here in Solway is the source of my blue jeans, but just because I like my jeans doesn't mean I like where I got them. That place is a pain in the ass, and I don't even go there anymore. Anyhow, I forgot about those blasted pictures. I should have warned you. I'm just so used to them. And so is Momma. Most of them she's had for years and years."

Aphra nodded. "I figured as much. Honestly, the pictures didn't bother me as much as how your mother acted. She made it clear that she doesn't see me as anyone important. Just a young chick you're getting your rocks off with. Nobody she cares to get to know."

"Now I'm going to say the same thing to you about my momma that you said to me about yours: give her a chance. Momma will like you as a person. You've got a dignity and a maturity about you that she's never seen in Norma, even if you are twenty years younger. And Momma will figure that out."

"Well, at least I don't expect as much drama with folks on my end." Aphra paused, thinking, then she said, "Speaking of which, I'd like to bring you to next Sunday's cookout at Di's. I want you to meet everyone."

"Will that Tony be there?"

"Probably. He's Trevor's best friend, so that makes him a de facto part of the family."

Isaac gave Aphra a level gaze. "I'll go, if that's what you want. But if I catch that Tony doing so much as looking sideways at you, I'll get him told real quick."

Aphra grinned, perversely glad that he was jealous. "Won't happen. Tony's not the sort of guy who'd take on another guy for a woman. He's a momma's boy something fierce. A lot like Sam, actually." She stopped herself short. "Oh, crap, I'm sorry. I shouldn't have said that."

"Don't apologize for being honest. I know what you meant."

"So what's the deal with Sam, anyway? He's a big boy, isn't he, married, a father-to-be, going on twenty-five years old? He acted like he liked me when I met him at your cabin. Now he's acting like I'm the enemy."

"Honey, Sam's a good boy and we get along fine, but as you've picked up on, he's more his mother's son than mine. He never wanted me to date anybody after the divorce, and he's never stopped saying little things to me about getting back together with his mother. He'd like you if he'd allow himself to, but for that to happen, he'll need to get out from under his mother's wing a little bit."

"What about Cheryl, his wife? How does she fit in?"

"She's like Norma."

"But she seems so quiet and mousy."

"She is quiet and mousy, and yeah, Norma's got a mouth on her like a siren. But they're the same type of woman under the surface: cold, manipulative and self-centered. They thrive on attention. Same song, different dance. I hate it for Sam. I really do. But it's what he's used to in women, it's what he grew up with."

"Be up front with me, Isaac. Are you sure spending time with me won't bring too much stress upon your head? You'll be dealing with aggravation all around: from Norma, from your mother, and from Sam. Do you really need that, at this point in your life?"

"What I need is you. And as for stress, that's a laugh. You're forgetting who you're talking to. Norma's shenanigans are nothing compared to a nest of NVA snipers. Remember that."

Aphra hoped he was right. Alas, doubt's gloomy specter kept tap-tapping on her mind's window.

14. Excrescence

"I'm not sure about this," Aphra said as Isaac parked his Scrambler in front of his cabin.

"It'll be okay."

"I'm really, really not sure about this." Aphra was a least five hundred megaparsecs shy of sure—a megaparsec being equivalent to just over three million light years.

"It's got to happen sometime," Isaac said, "and it might as well happen on my home turf. I say, bring it on. The sooner we nip it in the bud, the better."

"You could take me home first, though. I don't think I ought to be around for the fireworks if Norma and Sam do show up and things get ugly."

"But if I took you back to your place, I'd feel as if I were leaving you out in the cold. I don't want you to feel the way those pictures made you feel. You're becoming the center of my life, and I don't want you on the sidelines. And hey, what if they don't show up? I want us to spend the day together, not apart waiting for other people's shoes to drop."

Aphra appreciated his sentiment. But was this course of action the most sensible way to express it? She feared Isaac's well-intentioned efforts to protect her from hurt would only wind up causing her more hurt. But she couldn't bring herself to insist that Isaac take her home. If he wanted her there, she'd be there.

Maybe Norma and Sam wouldn't show up.

And maybe Isaac's impeccably maintained Scrambler wouldn't start next time he turned its key.

On entering Isaac's cabin, Aphra saw Hieu sitting at the kitchen table. He welcomed her and Isaac with a crinkly-faced grin of such wattage that she was compelled to blink. Maybe things would be okay. Not everyone in Isaac's life wished she'd disappear.

"Tell me, Aphra," Hieu said. "Do you have a sister, and is she available?"

"I have a younger sister, but she's an old, married lady."

"Too bad for me." Hieu looked at Isaac. "But oh so fortunate for you, Snake! And guess what. Though I'm unlucky in love, my luck might be changing for the better in another way."

"What's up?" Isaac asked.

"I might have a job."

"That software engineering thing?"

"Maybe. They were impressed with what I can do. If I get the job, I'll be making money again." The scar on Hieu's cheek puckered as his expression saddened. "And I need it. My savings is almost gone, and I have bills to pay to the family court. And I need to give you your house back."

Isaac patted Hieu on the back. "Don't worry about it, Swampy. You're to stay here as long as you need to."

Hieu looked at Isaac, at Aphra, then back at Isaac. "Do you two want to be alone? Maybe now would be a good time to go for my run."

"Yeah, it might be, but not for the reason you're thinking. Norma might show up."

"Norma!" Hieu's shocked expression verged on comical. "Why would she come, with you and Aphra here?"

"Long story. I don't know for sure that she's coming, but it's likely. Feel free to hang around, but if she comes, don't say I didn't warn you."

"No, no. I'll go for my run. I don't like to be around Norma. She's worse for my stomach than Tabasco sauce. That stuff is dangerous, Snake."

Isaac chuckled. "Suit yourself, bud. Have a good run."

After Hieu went out, Isaac said, "He's really something. Got a backbone like a saw log. But I'm worried that his problems are getting him down a lot more than he lets on."

"I hope things work out for him," Aphra said. "He's a good guy, and he deserves better than what he's had to deal with."

Fifteen minutes later, Aphra heard the click of heels on Isaac's flagstone walkway. A knock on the door followed. Isaac straightened his eyeglasses, squared his shoulders, and went to open the door.

Norma was alone. As she stood in the doorway, her manner was beseeching, though it hardened briefly when she spotted Aphra sitting at the kitchen table. "Sammy wanted to come with me," she told Isaac, "but he had to get Miss Maggie to take him back to the garage. He's got a busy day at work today. But it's just as well he didn't come. We can't plan his surprise party with him here, now can we?"

"Sam's birthday is going to be simple," Isaac said. "At one point, he'll spend time with you, and at another point, he'll spend time with me. We're divorced, Norma. Remember?"

"That's not how it was when he was born." She came in and seated herself in one of Isaac's wingback chairs, crossing her legs to show her stylish, high-heeled t-straps to their best advantage. "I've been doing some thinking, and seeing as how we have a brand new Lightfoot on the way, I just keep coming back to the importance of family. Family is everything. If you don't have family, then you don't have much." She shot another hard glance in Aphra's direction then continued speaking to Isaac. "I guess I've always thought you'd come home to me someday. Aren't you tired of our family being split? Don't you think it would be something really special to give our grandchild the gift of a united family, kind of the ultimate birthday present?"

"Shit," Isaac muttered. Then he folded his arms across his chest and regarded Norma as though he sought to pin her to the chair with his gaze. "Look, I'm sick of it, and I'm sick of you. You and I were never a family. A family is what's in your heart, what's in your mind. It's not what's on a piece of paper. We weren't a family when we were married, we aren't a family now, and we're never going to be a family. I'll always be civil to you, for Sam's sake. But you aren't my wife, and you aren't my family."

"I think Sammy would disagree about us not being a family," Norma said. "He's got pictures of you and me, with him as a baby and a young boy, hanging all over him and Cheryl's bedroom."

Sam, a twenty-five year-old man, plastered his marital bedroom with Mommy-Daddy-Baby pictures? Good grief.

"God knows, I never wanted Sam to be hurt," Isaac said. "Trouble is, though, he was hurt from the beginning of his life by our bad marriage. Remember how tense and unhappy our household was when we were married? The problem with you is that you see me striking out on a new path, and you have a terrible fear of change. You'd prefer to return to a comfortable misery with me than you would to make a new life for yourself, the life you should always have had."

"But if we put things together again, we could make it better," Norma insisted. "I still love you, you know. And it would be Sam's dream come true. And I shudder thinking about you, someday in the future, introducing some biker chick, her over there or another one like her, to our grandchildren as your wife. You're above that, you know. And our family deserves better."

Listening, Aphra swallowed hard. Their family. Not hers. It could never be hers. Again, she was the outsider, the excrescence, never belonging. Was she to endure this pattern all her life?

"I've heard your whiny bullshit all these years, and I've had enough." Isaac jabbed a finger in Norma's direction. "You don't love me, you don't really want me. You just don't want to fail. You couldn't care less who or what I married, or if I ever married anybody at all. This isn't about us. It's about you and your character as a human being. You've never developed your own self. And you can't live your life through me. So the simplest thing I can say— it might be a cliché, but it's very appropriate—is Norma, get a life. Because mine isn't yours."

Aphra's hands knit and unknit themselves in her lap as though they were independent of her cognitive functions. Why wasn't Isaac telling Norma that he neither loved nor wanted her? Did only Norma's feelings count? Or was there a remnant of him that did love Norma, did want Norma, or could under the right circumstances? Could he, deep inside, agree with Norma that he—that their family —deserved better than somebody like Aphra?

Norma slid out of the chair like a shamed dog. "Well, I'll go on now. I've said my piece. Give some thought to it. We could be family, a real family. It would be best for everybody. You know it would."

"You ask me to consider the matter as though I'd never considered it before. There wasn't a day that went by of our marriage that I didn't consider it. And for me, the issue is done, closed, and left way behind. And that's where you need to put it, too."

At Isaac's words, Aphra's gut churned like rocks in a tumbler. Worse than folly, it was downright arrogance on her part to assume that he could be anywhere near as committed and devoted to her as he had been, in the past, to Norma. What was Aphra doing here? Looking the fool, that was what.

Norma sidled up to Isaac and precisely echoed Aphra's thoughts. "If you loved me so much once, couldn't you love me again?"

He stepped away from her. "You know as well as I do that our marriage wasn't based on love. It was based on situations that were problems in our lives. We made a mistake. A mistake that lasted almost thirty years. Far too long. So let's not give it another second of our time. We've both got better things to do."

"Like running around with her? That Abra?"

"Yeah," Aphra grumbled. "Abra the Biker Chick with the stud through her tongue and the multiple labia piercings."

Norma shuddered theatrically.

"You wouldn't care whether it was Aphra or the Queen of England," Isaac said. "What you're doing, Norma, is you're playing a psychological game. You don't care about me, you care about winning the game. Everything to you has always been about winning the game. So I'm telling you flat-out, straight-out, and this is the way it is: the game is over. I don't play it anymore. The—game —is—over."

He staggered out his last four words like rounds of precisely aimed rifle fire, then he joined Aphra at the kitchen table. Aphra wondered why he didn't take her hand. There it was, just lying on the kitchen table. Why didn't he want to touch her in front of Norma?

Norma left without another word, then it was like Aphra had remembered how to breathe.

Norma was hypocritical, superficial, and rude. So why did Aphra feel sorry for her?

15. Afterthought

"Well, I'm glad she's gone." Aphra was the Mistress of Understatement. And Isaac still hadn't taken her hand. She moved it under the table to appease her wounded pride.

Isaac looked over at her, apparently jolted out of a reverie—about what, pray tell? "Yeah, I'm glad, too. That woman wears me out. I hope what I said is going to take." He looked closer at Aphra, and she wished she hadn't moved her hand. "You okay, Kitten?"

"I don't know whether I am or not. I'm feeling intimidated."

"By Norma?"

"By all of it." Watching Isaac slip into well-worn grooves of habit with his ex-wife had distilled from the fog of Aphra's mind the true, mammoth shape of Isaac and Norma's past relationship, which threatened to crush her fragile hope with its weight. Three decades was almost as long as Aphra had been alive. Wouldn't Isaac want Norma back if he felt she would meet him halfway, as she never did before? How could Aphra aspire to be, in his life, anything more than an afterthought—a brief, crisp breeze at the end of a long, hot day?

"All of what?" Isaac furrowed his brow.

And Aphra could no longer hold back her flood of words. "See, that's part of my problem right there, that you can even ask that. You're still so embroiled in old patterns with her that you can't see how things look to me. And whether you like it or not, you have a lifelong bond with Norma because you have a child with her. People who are important fixtures in your life have a vested interest in the two of you putting your family back together, even a baby who hasn't been born yet. Can't you see? I don't stand a chance here."

"And I'm double-dog damned if you aren't spouting the same kind of crap she did. What are you talking about, vested interest?

What sane human being has a vested interest in misery? And what do you mean, you don't stand a chance? Doesn't what I want count, or am I everybody else's puppet, strings jerking me to and fro, with no will of my own?"

"I didn't mean—"

"Sure, though," he interrupted, "you could hook up with somebody with less baggage then me, couldn't you, like that Tony. And I bet you're starting to think about that." He shifted his gaze from Aphra, to Hieu's empty chair.

"Oh, Isaac. That isn't at all what I meant."

"But it's the same difference, isn't it?" he said, his voice roughening. "You've seen there's going to be some rough sailing with me, and you want off my boat. If you can get me back in Norma's clutches, you won't have to deal with any of this shit. You could sail off into the sunset with some sissified little son of a bitch who won't give you any of the headaches you'll get from me. That's it, isn't it? That's what you're up to."

Aphra was startled. "No, sweetheart, no. I've fallen deeply in love with you. I want you as long as you want me. I would want you even if you didn't want me. What you're saying just isn't true."

Isaac rubbed his beard, and his big shoulders deflated like balloons. "Okay, I'm sorry. I know it isn't true. Now if I can only remember it. Man oh man, all this drama gets me talking crazy." Then he straightened up and looked into her eyes. "You aren't the only one who's got insecurities. And I'm sorry for mine. They flared up for a minute there, and I acted like a horse's ass."

"Well, you aren't any more of a horse's ass than I am."

"So talk to me. Get Norma off your chest so we can enjoy the rest of our day and not have to mention her again."

"Okay. I guess what's bugging me is this. From the way you talked to her, it sounded to me like you have feelings for her. Like you'd take her back if you could be sure that she'd meet you halfway."

"Now what the hell did I say to give you a crazy idea like that?"

"I think it's less what you said than what you didn't say. You pointed out to Norma that she doesn't love you and doesn't want you, but you never told her that you don't love or want her. And you kept reminding her that she never truly cared about you and that she still doesn't, as though that fact hurts you and always has."

"Oh," Isaac said. "I think I see."

"See what?"

"I think you wanted me to tell her that I can't stand her, to ride her out on a rail. And maybe you wanted me to get on her for putting you down the way she did."

"You're right," Aphra said.

"But don't you see? Love and hate are opposite sides of the same coin, both of them strong feelings that signify an emotional attachment for good or bad. And I have no emotional attachment to Norma. Since I have no emotional attachment to her, why would I want to engage her any more than I have to? What business is it of hers how I feel about anybody or anything in my life? Don't get me wrong. I resent how Norma talked about you, and I resent what she's trying to pull with Momma and Sam. But as far as Norma herself is concerned, I'm as indifferent to her as I'd be to a stick of firewood. True, I don't like her. But there are plenty of people in the world I don't like. I don't let them rent space in my head."

Aphra was still bothered that he hadn't taken up for her, but she changed the subject. "Well, aren't you worried about growing distant from Sam and the soon-to-be grandchild because of me? Do you want to wind up like Hieu? He misses his kids so much."

"Sam is grown, he makes his own decisions. And I have the right to choose my life just as he has the right to choose his. Sure, I want him to like you and feel comfortable around us, but he's going to do what he's going to do. That's just how life works. At any rate, I like to think he'd prefer seeing his dad happy instead of lonely or unhappy."

The tumbler was still agitating Aphra's stomach. She folded her hands on the table, not knowing what else to do. But Isaac dislodged one, raised it to his lips, and kissed it.

"I know this must be hard for you," he said. "Here I am, jealous of that Tony who's nothing to you or to your life while you're sitting here staring my thirty-year former marriage in the face. What you said about old patterns got to me. I'd never thought about that, and you're right. People are bound to create patterns, whether good or bad, over the course of three decades, and too many people fall into bad patterns for a lifetime. Norma and I weren't partners, companions, or friends. She was never a wife to me except on paper. And having a man's babies doesn't make a woman a wife. I saw Sam born, and I'm glad I did, but I have to admit to you that I didn't feel any more for Norma while it was happening than when I've watched cows in a barnyard having their calves. There's something deeply wrong with that. It wouldn't have been that way if it had been you, that's for sure."

At his words, Aphra's tumbler slowed its churning. She glanced up at him, and tears started in her eyes.

"Fact is," Isaac continued, "when Norma and I got married, we built a prison, not knowing any better. We were cell mates who reproduced. Then all three of us, parents and son, existed for decades in that prison. And enough is enough. Norma, Sam and I are lucky. We've been sprung from prison. Each one of us has a chance to create new patterns to replace the old. And my sweet Aphra, I hope … I pray I'm lucky enough to create my new patterns with you."

"That's what I want, too." Aphra's stomach had calmed and all she wanted was to hug Isaac. She got up, but he pulled her down on his lap and wrapped his arms around her. "God, how I love you. Please don't jump my ship because of a few scuttlebutts. It'll be okay. Damn it, I'll make it okay."

"And so will I." She rubbed her cheek against his beard, loving its bristly texture. Despite everything and everyone around them, Aphra felt she belonged when she was in Isaac's arms.

"Bear?" she said after a moment.

"Mmm?"

"I know something we can create together."

"What's that?"

She leaned back to look into his eyes. "A book, of course."

He stroked his mustache. "Hey, that's a good idea. Do you want to help me with that novel I'm starting about the old soldier falling in love for the first real time in his life?"

"Would that really be okay?" Realizing that she sounded like a child who had been offered a lifetime supply of bubble gum, Aphra couldn't help but laugh.

Isaac laughed, too, and touched her cheek. "Yeah. It would be more than okay. It's high time one of my books had a woman's perspective informing it. And I can't think of anybody's I'd rather have than yours. You're a fighter, too, you know."

"I guess so, in my weird way. One thing, though. Could you hold off sending for publication any novel we co-write until I've built up a few publishing credits of my own? I want to build my credits on the merit of my own work, not on the association of my name with yours. Do you understand? I haven't hurt your feelings, have I?"

"Lord God, no. That's fine with me. I admire your integrity."

Aphra was aglow. She couldn't believe she'd be working with Isaac Lightfoot on his new novel. And good grief, she simply had to can the groupie shit! There she sat on Isaac's lap with his arms around her, and she was still thinking of him as a remote, inaccessible figure. That just wouldn't do. Lover, mentor, friend —Isaac. How had she gotten so lucky?

Isaac's hand was under her hair, caressing her neck, and the yearning in his eyes prickled her from her inmost center out to the tips of her fingers and toes. Sitting in his lap, she felt outlined in stark relief the urgency of his desire—he was rock hard!—and when she wiggled down against him, he made a low noise in his throat.

"You'd better not do that, unless you want me to take you right now, on the floor, on the bed over there, against the wall, or any damn place. But Hieu could come home any minute."

"Then it's a pity we aren't exhibitionists," she said hotly against his lips while wiggling down on him again.

Aphra wondered what expression Hieu had worn when he entered the cabin to find Isaac and herself gone from his sight with vigorous thumps and moans coming from the bathroom, the only walled enclave in the cabin. But Hieu's black eyes were dancing when she and Isaac emerged, hand-in-hand, to join him at the kitchen table, and all three of them were blushing hot as sun-ripened tomatoes.

16. Vaguely-Female Shape

Aphra couldn't help herself: she had to read it again. It was the substance of things hoped for in more ways than one, for *Substance of Things Hoped For* was the title of their novel. The chapter she held was their love fused and made manifest, part of each of them yet separate from both of them, for the first time.

And besides that, the chapter was good.

Today, it resided in Aphra's office, but throughout the past week it had been labored over, interspersed with Isaac's projects and her Web jobs, both here and at Isaac's cabin—whichever place, on a given day, was most conducive to creativity.

Aphra left her office and joined Isaac at the kitchen table. "I read it again."

Isaac held Pilar on his lap. He scratched her fuzzy chin and grinned at Aphra. "I figured. My writing style and yours fit together like peanut butter and strawberry jelly, don't they?"

"I'd say."

"And if we do what we did this week, say, thirty more times, then it'll be our novel we're reading over and over again."

With her finger, Aphra traced the outline of the snake tattoo on his upper arm. "I like the sound of that. Our novel."

"I do, too," he said.

"Speaking of things that are 'ours,' I guess you ought to move 'our' cat off your lap so we can go to the cookout." As the purring Pilar leaned her face into Isaac's hand, Aphra added, "Perhaps instead of 'our' cat, I should say 'your' cat."

Isaac chuckled. "It's more like she's decided that I'm her person."

"She has indeed claimed you in the name of Catdom," Aphra agreed, though Old Man Santiago was fond of Isaac, too. Though at first, Santiago was suspicious of a male newcomer to his realm, he now bestowed upon Isaac plenty of ankle rubs and friendly meows.

Isaac stroked the hair bracelet on his wrist. He hadn't taken it off since Aphra had tied it there two weeks before. Then he moved Pilar from his lap and stood up. The cat trotted off into the living room, no doubt in search of a coffee stirrer on the verge of wreaking its plastic cylindrical menace upon unwitting humanity, a threat perceptible only to ever-vigilant, orange fluff balls.

Aphra loved riding with Isaac on his bike: putting her arms around him, leaning into his back, and surrendering to the turns and dips as he executed them, he, she, and the bike as one. It was open-air lovemaking, the most fun they could have with their clothes on. And Hermes himself, were he plucked from myth and rendered in flesh, couldn't pilot a Harley more skillfully than did Isaac. It was as if the motorcycle became an extension of his body, control of its speed and power as effortless as the maintenance of his heartbeat and respiration.

Di and Trevor's house was a brick rancher, plain and snug, enhanced by a profusion of red tulips and yellow daffodils out front. Though they weren't late, Isaac and Aphra were last to arrive, judging by the three vehicles already parked in the driveway. Isaac untied his Outback hat from his bike's sissy bar, settled it on his head, and hand-in-hand, he and Aphra made their way to the back yard and the patio.

Trevor, moist and red-faced, squirted lighter fluid onto a stack of charcoal briquettes that had been piled up in the patio grill. Bodhi reclined in a lawn chair reading a book. Mom bustled around Di's picnic table laying out tableware, paper plates, and napkins, and Di bustled alongside her, placing serving spoons into bowls laden with food and opening bags of buns. Benches on either side of the table provided seating, and Tony sat at the table, watching the action unfold.

He got up and approached Isaac and Aphra. "Are you the Isaac Lightfoot I've heard so much about?"

"I guess which Isaac Lightfoot I am depends on what you've heard. But yeah, that's my name." He offered Tony his hand. Faced with Isaac's size and presence, Tony was dwarfed, and after shaking Isaac's hand, he stepped back a couple of paces as though trying to compensate for his lesser gravity with increased distance.

"I'm Tony Farthing. Friend of the family. I've known Trevor since we were kids."

"Some friends are like family, aren't they?" Isaac said. "I've got a couple of those myself."

Tony ambled back to the picnic table as Di and the Earth Mother finished their tasks. Looking more like sisters than like mother and daughter, they approached Isaac and Aphra, arm-in-arm.

"Your bike sounds different, Alf," Di said. "Quieter."

"Isaac and I rode over here on his bike."

Di and Mom looked at Isaac, who explained, "Aphra's bike's got straight pipes, but mine's got a factory muffler. Aphra likes that rumble, but my ears are about rumbled out."

Having finally lit the charcoal, Trevor joined them. "Guess you heard enough loud noise in Vietnam to last a lifetime, huh?"

"Heavy artillery and machine gun fire wear on a man's ears pretty quick."

"This is Trevor, Di's husband," Aphra told Isaac. "You've already met Mom. And over there sits Larry, my daddy. Daddy! Get your nose out of that book, for the love of Pete, and come on over here."

Bodhi, as usual, was oblivious to the hubbub that surrounded him as he read. As a child, Aphra thought comic-book aliens from Zeta Reticuli could land five feet away from her father, emerge from their silver space ship which would resemble a living-room light fixture, extend their obligatory suckered tentacles toward Bodhi, and as long as he was absorbed in a book, he'd never notice them until he found their unspeakable appendages wrapped around his neck, ready to penetrate his facial orifices, liquefy his vital organs, and slurp them out for food. And his last words would likely be: "Before you do me in, let me finish reading this page."

"Yo, Bodhi!" Aphra shouted again for good measure.

Hearing her latest exhortation, the Bodhisattva looked up from his tome, mild surprise on his face.

"Oh, I'm sorry." He put his book on the chair and joined them. "Isaac Lightfoot, huh? Though I haven't read all your books like Alf here, I've read quite a few of them. You're a fine writer."

"You're very kind," Isaac said, shaking Bodhi's hand.

The Earth Mother eyeballed the hair bracelet on Isaac's wrist. "I have to admit, I wish Alf didn't like motorcycles so much. They're so dangerous, especially in the city with all the traffic."

"That reminds me," Aphra said. "I know what I want for Christmas, when it rolls around."

"What?" Mom asked.

"I want you to go to that custom T-shirt place in the mall and have them make me a T-shirt that says, 'Organ Donation Courtesy of Harley-Davidson.'"

Isaac's lips twitched in amusement, and Mom frowned. "Alf! That's not funny."

Di whacked Aphra's shoulder. "Quit picking on Mom. Come to the kitchen and help me carry out the hamburgers and hot dogs, okay?"

"All right, if I must," Aphra said playfully. "Daddy, try not to talk Isaac into a stupor about modern philosophy, okay?"

Daddy looked at Isaac. "Say, that reminds me. Have you ever studied phenomenology? I've picked up on elements in the thematic structure of your novel, *The Lion and the Cobra*, that suggest familiarity with certain precepts of Merleau-Ponty's philosophy, specifically where you seem to champion alternatives to ontological dualism."

Isaac's eyes widened. "Whoa. I never thought anybody would notice that." He winked at Aphra, and with tremendous effort, she restrained a spate of giggles.

Only Bodhi would glean such a thing from *The Lion and the Cobra*, an edgy novel that chronicled the struggles of a young American medic after his return home from Vietnam. Written in psychedelic first-person narrative, it veered back and forth between sketches of postwar distress and flashbacks to the field, both of which were flagged by song lyrics of the two periods. From woolly bullies to whiter shades of pale, it was quite a ride.

Aphra accompanied Di to her kitchen where two trays awaited them, one filled with hot dogs and the other filled with ground beef shaped into patties.

"Good God, Alf." Di's eyes were bright. "I wouldn't give a hoot if Isaac Lightfoot was a hundred and fifty years old and had forty ex-wives and a hundred kids. He's hot, plain and simple."

Aphra burst out laughing. "I guess this means you like him, huh?"

"I sure do. I hope his ex-wife leaves you alone, though. What if she tries to kill you or something?"

"She won't. Besides, even if she did, I could stomp her butt into the ground."

"Sure you could." It was hard to tell whether or not Di was being sarcastic.

They carried the trays outside and turned them over to Trevor, then he and Di began laying hot dogs and beef patties onto the grill. Mom and Tony watched as Aphra rejoined Daddy and Isaac, who were engrossed in conversation.

"In my opinion, it's the conflict theorists who are correct," Isaac said. "The overriding factor in the shaping of society is power and who holds it."

"I don't know," Bodhi said, narrowing his eyes thoughtfully. "I'm more of a functionalist myself. People who share values work for the good of the whole. To discount the impact of cooperation in shaping society is to ignore the better part of our nature as human beings."

"But we must distinguish individual proclivities from group dynamics," Isaac insisted. "It's apples versus oranges. Sure, people can be altruistic. My fellow soldiers in Vietnam would have died for me and I for them, but it can't be denied that the puppet masters of war operate from selfish motives. What I'm saying about society in the main, though, is this: if man put an end to war, he'd be extinct within a hundred years."

"I'll bite," Daddy offered. "Why do you say that?"

"Because the planet itself would kill us. Bacteria and viruses would rise, and there would be no way to fight them. Our greatest technological advances, medicine, so many things that have improved the length and quality of human life, have come about, by and large, not because of altruism but because of war. Every life form on this planet must fight to survive, and we're no different. War is never pretty. In fact, it's downright rotten. But when I look at the big picture, I see that war checks humanity and strengthens us." Isaac smiled wryly and added, "Of course, being an old soldier, I'm not exactly a prime candidate for adherence to functionalism."

Bodhi nodded. "I can't say I agree with you, but you've made me think."

"You've strayed quite a ways from philosophy, haven't you?"

Aphra asked.

"Well, I've been interested in sociology and anthropology for a number of years," Isaac said. "So I figured I'd ask your dad for his take on the split between sociology's two main theoretical perspectives on the macroscopic level."

"All right," Mom called from the table. "Save the egghead talk for dessert. Give our stomachs a chance to whet an appetite."

Daddy grinned at her. "Who's an egghead?" He went to sit beside her at the table.

Trevor announced that the meat was ready, and they served themselves, both from the grill and from the table. Di and Mom had prepared macaroni salad, baked beans, and slaw, and there were potato chips and corn chips in baskets. Beside the table was a cooler full of drinks, and after they'd filled their plates and taken a can of soda each, Mom and Daddy seated themselves on one side of the table, and Trevor and Di seated themselves on the other. Aphra scooted in beside Di, but as she did, a red-faced Tony scooted in next to her, forcing Isaac to take a seat with Bodhi and the Earth Mother on the other side of the table. Was that satisfaction Aphra saw on her mother's face? Had she told Tony to do that? Tony was gazing at his plate.

Aphra glanced at Isaac, whose jaw was tight and whose visage was rife with storm clouds. When she rolled her eyes at him to express her displeasure, the lines of his jaw eased up.

Eating commenced, and no one said anything for several minutes. Then Mom spoke up. "Did you get plenty, Di? Remember, dear, you're eating for two."

"For two?" Trevor said. "You ought to see her raid the refrigerator when she gets up in the morning. You'd think she's incubating a whole classroom. And oh, what she eats! It turns my stomach. Cucumber and mustard sandwiches, sardines dipped in chocolate sauce..."

Di socked Trevor on the arm. "Hush, you."

"And Tony, how are things going coaching that tee ball team?" Mom asked. "Are you having fun?"

"Oh, yeah," Tony exclaimed, brightening. "I'm having a blast with those little guys."

"I bet they love you to death," Mom said.

"Not meaning to brag, but yeah, they do."

"Children are such a joy," Mom said. "How old is your son, Isaac?"

"He'll be twenty-five a week from this coming Thursday. He works long hours in his garage on weekdays, so we're celebrating his birthday the weekend after next."

"You and your ex-wife are throwing a party for him, then? How nice."

Isaac scowled. "No, the ex is doing her own thing. I'm taking Sam and his wife out to eat. My mother's coming, and I'm hoping to have Aphra with us."

"Well, I'm sure it'll be a happy occasion," Mom said. "I've always thought that parenthood is the most fulfilling and rewarding thing people can do with their lives. Having a child of your own, Isaac, I'm sure you must agree."

Isaac said nothing. Of course he didn't. What could he possibly say? If he agreed with Mom, then he'd trivialize his connection to Aphra and would concede that he sought to deny her Life's Most Fulfilling and Rewarding Experience. If he disagreed with Mom, then he'd trivialize his connection to his son. He couldn't win. Damn it, Mom, Aphra thought. Why are you doing this?

It was coming out, Aphra couldn't stop it. "Happily, in this day and time, parenthood isn't compulsory. It's a choice. In our overpopulated world, reason dictates that a woman ought to feel free to aspire to loftier heights than reproduction which is, after all, an act which any mere bug can perform."

Mom glared at her. "What an ugly thing to say."

"It isn't ugly. It's practical. Not everybody is into kids, and not everybody should feel forced to go against their natural inclinations. Instead of broadening my belly, I'd rather broaden my mind. Some of us want to do other things with our lives, you know."

"Like what? Designing Web sites for local grocers? Running the roads on a motorcycle all hours of the night? Figuring out some practical way to use that English degree of yours?"

An ironic comment, Aphra thought, from somebody who married a philosophy professor. "Sure, why not? I might start sculpting nude figures out of ear wax. It isn't for you to say what blows someone else's skirt up, Mom." Though her voice rang with bravado, the old pain seized her gut and twisted hard. And Aphra was damned if she'd let Mom see it. Why was it Aphra Mom picked at? Was getting pregnant an uncommon feat of mind, character, or skill? Unlike Di, Aphra had put herself through college on a full scholarship. And though Di had majored in accounting, she was the manager of a hole-in-the-mall clothing store, at the beck and call of corporate bosses. At least Aphra was her own boss.

And what the bleeding effigies had the Earth Mother done, besides birthing and raising her Golden Girl and one other, a shabby creature of vaguely-female shape who registered, once in a great while, on the radar of her heart's periphery?

None of that mattered, though. What mattered was this: it was Di, not Aphra, who toed Mom's line. Who always had, and who always would.

Aphra looked across the table at Isaac. He was frowning. He knew Mom had hurt her.

Di, Mrs. Social Grease, slid to the rescue. "Tony, you ought to make working with kids your full-time vocation, as much as you enjoy them."

"I keep telling him that he ought to go to college and get his teacher's certification," Trevor said.

"I'm thinking about it," Tony said. "I guess it's taken me a while to figure out what I want to be when I grow up."

"It happens," Di said. "Nothing wrong with that."

To Isaac, Trevor said, "I bet you knew you wanted to be a soldier from the time you could talk."

"You'd be betting right. My daddy was a World War II vet and proud as punch of his service. Some of my first memories are of sitting on Daddy's lap while he told me war stories. I joined the Army pretty much right out of high school."

The Earth Mother glanced fondly at Bodhi. "We met in college, my first year there, and married when I graduated. We were a tie-dyed hippie couple, I'm afraid. And Larry got a draft card his junior year, which was his first year working on his Master's Degree. He received a deferment and didn't have to go to Vietnam. I don't mean any offense, Isaac, because I know you were quite a soldier, but I'm glad things worked out the way they did. Larry's a gentle spirit, like Tony here. I can't imagine someone like Larry surviving on the battlefield."

Daddy raised an eyebrow. "What do you mean by 'someone like me?'"

"Don't be so quick to judge," Isaac said to Mom. "It isn't always the aggressive, gung-ho guys who make the best soldiers. John, a member of my Ranger team and one of my best friends, was a lot like your husband. He was quiet, intellectual. He became a medical researcher after the war. And in 'Nam, he was one hell of a good soldier. He was awarded the Bronze Star for valor twice. And did you know that many of the Special Forces guys have advanced degrees in a wide range of subjects, including anthropology and linguistics?"

Bodhi smiled at Isaac. In his round spectacles, he made Aphra think of an owl.

Tony piped up. "Well, I'd have a hard time shooting another human being."

"You wouldn't if they were shooting at you," Isaac said. "You do what you have to do, so you and your buddies can go home in one piece."

Aphra could stand it no longer. "Excuse me, Tony. I need to get out of here."

He obliged her. She did have to use Di's bathroom. But when she returned to the picnic table, she walked around to Isaac's side and scooted in beside him, so close that their legs touched.

"Do you want your place back?" Tony asked.

"No, I'm fine over here," she said as Isaac put his arm around her shoulders. Di was smiling again, and even Trevor looked amused. Aphra was glad she couldn't see the expression on the Earth Mother's face. She knew it would only piss her off more.

For the remainder of the meal, Aphra didn't have much to say. Neither, she noticed, did Isaac. Neither ate much more, either. Adrift in a stream of baby name banter and tee ball talk, they smiled and nodded where necessary until, pleading fatigue, they jumped ashore and took their leave.

Back at Aphra's condo, they seated themselves on the loveseat. Aphra felt better being at home with Isaac and her cats, but Isaac took off his glasses, lowered his face to his hands, and let out a long breath that caused his shoulders to slump forward.

"Bear? What's wrong?" she asked as Pilar sauntered into the living room and threw herself, literally, at his feet.

He lifted his head and looked at Aphra. In the space of a few seconds, his expression had gone slack, its animation drained away like blood from a wound. "I'm having a spell of feeling bad. Don't pay any attention to me. I'll pass."

"Is it something someone said at the cookout?"

"No. Not really."

"Is it me?"

"No. It isn't anything or anybody."

"I don't understand."

"I'm sorry, I forget you haven't seen me like this. Honey, I've suffered from severe depression for years. Decades. For a long time, I self-medicated with whiskey. I don't do that anymore, but I still struggle mightily from time to time. My doctor prescribed pills that help to some extent, but there isn't anything that makes the low points go away completely. I just have to ride them out."

Aphra rubbed Isaac's back, making slow, easy circles. "Do you mean that you feel sad all the time, even when to other people you seem to be doing okay?"

"No. Sometimes I feel fine. By severe depression, I mean that my problems with depression have been long term, and in all likelihood it isn't going anywhere. But as long as I keep myself busy through the bad days, I can weather it. Writing helps. And working in my shop. And spending time with you helps the most. You're the best medicine I've ever had."

She wanted to ask him something but wasn't sure how. "Do you... do you ever think..."

"About suicide?"

"Yes. That."

"I couldn't do it. I'm determined to live, to thrive. And you recollect what I've written about in my books: never give misfortune more than what it takes, and—"

She gently interrupted. "—and learn to love the ride. Oh, yes. Those words have helped me in my own life more than you could know."

"See there?" He patted her knee. "If nothing else, I'm a cussed old son of a bitch, and I'm not good at giving up. I guess anybody, if he's got a working brain and he's lived long enough, is carrying some kind of demon in his rucksack. And when he thinks too hard about the weight of the demon, that's when it drags him down."

"I think I know what you mean."

Santiago jumped into Aphra's lap, and Isaac lowered his head into his hands again and jittered his leg up and down, up and down, creating a tiny earthquake. And together, Aphra and Isaac waited for an unseen hand, whether of divine or biochemical origin, to lift him out of his dark void.

He'd told Aphra that she was good medicine. But how could that be, if by encouraging him to make a place for her in his life and to take his place in hers, she was only compounding his problems?

17. Dug Up and Pulverized

"Bear?" Aphra said.

Her head was pillowed on Isaac's shoulder following a round of luscious Saturday afternoon lovemaking. The only thing she wore was the bracelet he'd given her the night before: a slender gold circle accented by two intertwined hearts. Santiago curled around Isaac's head and Pilar, as always, commanded his feet, her head cushioned on his real foot and her body draped over his prosthesis as though she were a boneless cat.

"Yes, honey?" Isaac said, stroking her back.

"Maybe it would be best if I didn't go with you this evening."

"I don't want to hear that again."

"Norma will be there."

"No, she won't. I'm paying for supper, and I told Sam that he's not to bring his mother."

"He didn't like that, did he?"

"Doesn't matter. I'm his father."

She digested this. Then she said, "Nobody but you wants me there."

"Hieu wants you there."

"Okay, nobody besides you and Hieu."

He looked over at her. "Hang in there with me, okay?"

"I am, I am. But tonight will be stressful, and don't you think you should try to minimize your stress? You've been having those awful dreams almost every night now, waking me up yelling orders. You talk to me like I'm one of your men." But that wasn't the worst. The worst was the wordless, soundless sobs.

"Don't worry about it. I have to deal with those dreams every now and again. At least when I wake up, I've got you there beside me."

"Why won't you talk to me about them?"

"No reason to because they're all the same. Humping mile after mile through some blasted jungle with my foot full of shit and my body full of holes, fighting NVA regulars every step of the way and my buddies dying all around me. And I just keep going. I keep going when everybody else is dying, and none of it stops. And I know that it'll never stop, that I'll be bleeding and rotting and humping across the scorched face of the earth even when it's nothing but a dead, dark cinder. Nothing new under the sun."

"But there is, though. There's something else."

"No."

"Tell me."

He said nothing.

"Please."

He looked at Aphra, and she started at the sight of tears in his eyes. "It isn't only my buddies I can't save. Sometimes it's you. And I feel like it's my mistakes that did you in."

She held him close. "I'm okay. Please believe that. I'm doing the best I can. It's just hard, you know? Not with you and me, but with everything—everyone—else."

"I know. But as long as we both love and want each other, things will work out."

For a short while, they kissed and caressed each other, needing no words, cherishing the integrity of their world, his and hers alone. Aphra wished it could always be this way.

Alas, in the real world, a skirmish loomed on the horizon, and the time of engagement drew near.

Aphra kissed Isaac's snake tattoo, then she raised her head to look into his eyes. "As much as I'd love to stay here and snuggle, we'd better get up and get ready."

"I guess so," he said.

They reached the restaurant where they were to meet everyone, a buffet-style establishment Isaac chose to cater to the diverse tastes of their party. And there, among the throng of people standing in the lobby, Aphra was brought up short by Sam's frosty mien. He wore new, dark blue jeans, and behind him lurked Cheryl, who was doing a slightly better job of filling out her maternity dress than she had when Aphra had first seen her. Aphra smiled, but Cheryl only stared, her gaze bland and listless.

Isaac and Aphra both said hello.

Sam fixed his gaze on Isaac. "Hi, Dad. They're getting our table ready. It's a good thing you called in a reservation or else we'd be standing here for the next hour."

"Nobody else has made it yet?"

Sam looked at his watch. "It's only five 'til."

"Well, happy birthday, son. Here's a little something for you." He handed Sam an envelope. "You might want to use it to buy a wire feed welder so I can have mine back."

Sam smiled and tore open the envelope. Inside the envelope was a card and cash. The card was signed by both Isaac and Aphra. That hadn't been Aphra's idea – she hadn't wanted to push things with Sam. Isaac, however, had insisted.

Sam read the card then handed it to Cheryl, who tucked it in her purse. "Thanks, Dad."

"Lightfoot, party of six," called a hostess. "Your table's ready."

Sam, Cheryl, Isaac, and Aphra the Invisible Woman followed the hostess to a table in an alcove, situated at the end of the buffet. The buffet offered fare from salad to soup, hamburgers to salmon steaks, rolls to garlic bread, and practically every vegetable and dessert imaginable within the scope of American culinary ingenuity. If nothing else, they could all eat well. Isaac took the seat which looked out over the crowded room. Aphra sat on Isaac's left side, Sam sat on his right, and Cheryl sat on Sam's other side. Isaac draped his arm along Aphra's back and twined his fingertips through her hair. She took comfort in his touch. To him, she was real; that was what mattered.

Hieu hurried to their table and sat in the chair beside Aphra. "Happy birthday, Sam."

"Thanks, Uncle Hieu," Sam replied.

When Aphra smiled at Hieu, he returned her smile with interest and gave her hand a pat. "I see an empty chair. I guess I'm not too late."

"No buddy, you're right on time." A smile banished the tense lines of Isaac's face. Last night, he'd told Aphra that she, Hieu, and Greg were the only people in his life whose mere presence was able to soothe him. Hieu likes me, Aphra reminded herself. Isaac had said Greg would like her, too, and that John would also have liked her had he lived to meet her.

The thought reassured Aphra. After all, those men were his family, too.

Maggie blew in on a breeze of rose sachet which matched her pink polyester skirt and sat between Hieu and Cheryl. "Sorry I'm late. All that traffic, you know. But then I'm not exactly setting any speed records these days, either." She smiled at Sam. "I've already given Sam his present. Those jeans he's wearing."

"And I like them a bunch," Sam said. "Thanks again, Ma-maw. I needed 'em."

"He won't hardly spend a penny on new clothes, or on much of nothing else either except tools," Cheryl said. "And car parts."

A waitress took orders for drinks, and Isaac told her to put six buffets on one ticket. When everyone had returned to the table with full plates, Sam said, "Momma's having a party for me tomorrow, Dad. She said for me to tell you you're welcome to come. I told her I didn't think you'd take her up on it, though."

"Well, you thought right," Isaac said then took a bite of country fried steak.

"But Ma-maw will be there, won't you, Ma-maw?"

"I sure will," Maggie said enthusiastically.

Aphra's grilled chicken balled up in her mouth, but she tried to appear nonchalant. She accepted that Sam's attitude was what it was; she accepted that Maggie's attitude was what it was. And she accepted that there was nothing she could do to change either one. So why did it still hurt so much?

Isaac moved his hand under the table and put it on her knee.

"Say, Aphra," Hieu said, a fried shrimp perched between two of his fingers. "How did you learn to do such nice Web pages? I checked out Snake's new site, and I was impressed."

A lump formed in Aphra's throat. Had she grown so accustomed to barbs that the gentle touch of a feather made her cry? But when she spoke, her voice was steady. "I taught myself. I was blown away by the concept of the World Wide Web back in 1993, and I jumped on the HTML bandwagon before there was much graphical content to speak of. I guess you could say my Web skills have developed right alongside the Web itself."

"You can program in straight HTML, then?" Hieu asked. "Without relying on a WYSIWYG editor?"

"Sure can. Of course the Web design software I use has the

option of working in a WYSIWYG editor, straight code, or a split screen between the two, so I can modify source code when I'm dealing with nit-picky bugs that can't be fixed any other way."

"It's good to talk to a fellow computer nerd," Hieu said. "I like to work on Web pages, too, but I don't have your aesthetics. I'm not even good at taking pictures."

"Oh, man." Sam smiled a brittle smile. "Pictures. How could I forget? Cheryl, get me those pictures out of your purse."

Cheryl retrieved a manila envelope which Sam plucked eagerly from her fingers. He pulled out two photographs which he held up for the benefit of Maggie, who smiled in recognition. Then, to Isaac, Sam said: "Momma thought you might like to have these. They were taken, oh, about twenty-five years ago, give or take."

Isaac took them, and as he did, Aphra lay her fork on her plate and knitted her cold fingers in her lap. The top picture featured a young Norma, turned to the side and posing against a background of green lawn. Her enormous belly jutted out as though it were straining to free itself from the unfortunate pink jumper she wore. The hardness in her eyes as she smiled for the camera—pray tell, for Isaac?—on that long-ago day matched the hardness in her son's eyes as he watched Aphra for her reaction to the picture.

And as she lived and breathed, she wouldn't give him one.

Aphra met his gaze without hesitation. "Your mom looks like she was a happy pregnant lady."

He nodded, plainly taken aback. "Oh, she was. She loved being pregnant."

"Yeah, right," Isaac said. "You sure wouldn't have guessed it by the way she acted." He slapped the picture face-down on the table, revealing the second photo. It depicted a sweaty-faced Norma, covered up by blankets in what looked like a hospital bed, with a freshly-swaddled newborn on her chest. A young, tired-looking Isaac stood beside the bed. And images flowed into Aphra's mind: of Norma, naked, drenched in sweat, her legs spread wide and her feet in stirrups, her belly huge, round, and low. Of Isaac, stooped expectantly between her legs, pressing his hands against her inner thighs to help her bear down hard as she labored. Her groans, her sharp cries. His exhortations to push, push! Norma grunting, panting, moaning. Push! Panting, moaning, sobbing: push! Then, oh then, the crowning. Norma screaming in agony as her vagina stretched beautifully, no tearing. The blood-smeared head emerging, the moment nigh at hand. Screaming, sobbing: push! The shoulders. Push! The baby born and in its father's hands. Norma and Isaac's baby. Theirs. Norma's tears of agony changed to tears of joy.

Aphra felt a tear beside her nose, but it wasn't one of joy. She wiped it away, hoping no one saw it.

"—such a cute baby," Cheryl was saying.

"I remember taking that picture," Maggie said. "Your mother looks lovely, doesn't she? There's no moment a couple can share that's anywhere near as sweet."

Aphra let out a breath and counted to ten. To fifteen. To twenty. She wouldn't let them see that they'd got to her. She wouldn't let them see that they'd got to her. She wouldn't. Let them. See that they'd. Got to. Her. Would. Not.

But she thought she already had.

Her hands, still in her lap, were balled into fists. She stared at her plate. Green beans, cut off and sterile, to be devoured then excreted. Mashed potatoes, roots dug up and pulverized, never to flower. Grilled, seasoned chicken, meat which hatched from an egg, warm but dead. All women had eggs, though some women didn't use them. And another woman had used hers with the man Aphra loved.

Why were they all so quiet? Maybe they weren't quiet; maybe they were still talking. Maybe they were being shouted down by the brouhaha in her head.

She started at a soft touch on her hand. Hieu. Aphra couldn't look at him. Having an ally threatened to bring her tears to the fore, and she redoubled her efforts at control. It was easier to be hard-nosed when surrounded by hostiles.

Isaac wasn't a hostile. He loved her.

But he was once at the nexus of the enemy camp: between Norma's spreading thighs.

"Here, Sam." Isaac's voice was gruff. What was the matter with him? Were visions overcoming him as well, tender memories of the Mommy-Daddy-Baby Moments that he and Norma had shared? "I've got pictures of you as a little guy. They're what's important to me. I don't need or want pictures of your mother. Keep these, okay?" He put the pictures back into the envelope and handed it to

Sam, who accepted it reluctantly.

"I don't know why you won't keep them. Is it because of her?" He gestured toward Aphra.

"No. Aphra has nothing to do with it. I simply don't have a need to keep pictures of your mother. You ought to know that by now. And I won't play her games. I told her that, and I meant it. But I will say this." He looked first at Sam and Cheryl, then at Maggie. "Have any of you considered the possibility that Aphra has feelings, too?"

Sam studied Aphra as though she were a robot, a steel and spring creature, its behavior governed by circuits arranged on a board. "Well, if stuff like those pictures bothers her, then she shouldn't be involved with a man who already has a family."

Cheryl nodded.

Maggie nodded, too.

Hieu just looked sad.

And as though they were walls, their faces closed in on Aphra. She had to get away.

The restrooms were located behind Aphra, Isaac, and Hieu; they were in view of Sam, Cheryl, and Maggie. Aphra could plead nature's call and sneak out the restaurant's emergency exit without Isaac or Hieu seeing her, walk next door to the gas station, and use her cell phone to call a cab to take her home. Sam, Cheryl, and Maggie would be more than happy to see her go.

"Excuse me," Aphra muttered to no one in particular. She went into the women's bathroom and sequestered herself in a stall. For ten minutes, she sat on the john like Rodin's Thinker, with her chin cupped in her hand, but then, from the fog of her mind, her plan to sneak out re-emerged. If she took too long, Isaac would wonder where she was, and she needed to be well on her way home before he started wondering about anything.

But wait.

She couldn't leave.

She'd promised Isaac she'd hang in there with him, and she didn't break her promises. And he'd be hurt if she bolted. The last thing she wanted to do was to hurt her bear.

He'd taken up for her in front of all of them. At his son's birthday celebration, of all days.

Tears spilled from her eyes, and she seized a wad of toilet paper and wiped them away. She loved Isaac. And because she did, she had no choice. She couldn't retreat. She had to hold the line.

By the time she'd calmed down and washed her face, she'd been in the bathroom for twenty minutes, and when she made her way out, Isaac and Hieu were turned sideways in their seats, watching for her. How foolish she'd been, to have supposed that an old Army Ranger and an old Kit Carson Scout wouldn't notice her studying her perimeter, planning an escape route. Isaac's blustery eyes stared out of a mask, but when he saw Aphra, the mask shattered and all she saw was relief.

Aphra rejoined Lightfoot, Party of Six, and Isaac put his arm close around her. Hieu gave her a warm smile then focused on his apple pie. Sam, Cheryl, and Maggie were huddled in conversation about babies to come, but at least they weren't reminiscing about those from the past. The envelope containing the pictures was nowhere in sight. Was it something Isaac had said? No matter. Tension released Aphra from its cruel grip, and in its wake, she was played out. Used up. Spent.

"Honey, your supper's gotten cold," Isaac said. "Why don't you get another plate?"

"I don't want chicken, green beans, or potatoes."

"Well, there's other stuff."

"I know." She paused in thought then said, "I'll tell you what. Here in a few, I'll get a big slab of chocolate cake and ice cream with chocolate chips."

"That's my girl," Isaac said.

18. Unshakable Nexus

Aphra and Isaac sat in his wingback chairs, brainstorming their novel, but inspiration was hard to come by when she was worried Norma would call again.

That morning, at Aphra's condo, Isaac's cell phone had rung as he was making a beeline for the coffee pot. He'd had a bad night, another nightmare of bloody combat after which he couldn't get back to sleep. Aphra hadn't heard his conversation with Norma —she'd escaped to the shower.

At least Norma hadn't shown up at Isaac's cabin. Isaac had said she wouldn't, since she was throwing her birthday party for Sam today. And since the lawn was being mowed at Aphra's condo complex, Isaac's cabin was the best place for them to get some work done. Noisy lawnmowers drowned out Calliope's murmurings far more effectively than did the unlikely prospect of ex-wives arriving unannounced. And on such a beautiful Sunday afternoon, neither Isaac nor Aphra could resist embarking on the requisite bike ride to get over there—Isaac on his bike, Aphra on hers.

Though they had been invited to Di's cookout, they'd declined. Isaac was struggling under the weight of his demon and wanted to keep busy.

"—third-generation Japanese-American," he was saying.

"I'm sorry, what?"

"I'm warming up to your idea of making Carol a third-generation Japanese-American, since Henry fought in the Battle of Guadalcanal. I think it'll work, as long as we don't turn it into a ham-handed political soapbox of some sort."

"Uh-huh." Aphra had heard what he said, but it didn't register. He may as well have told her he wanted Carol to be a tentacled alien from Zeta Reticuli.

Isaac tapped his pencil on his notepad and studied Aphra over the top of his glasses. There were dark circles under his eyes. "Where are you, Aphra? Talk to me."

Aphra had been staring at the Tennessee Long Rifle hanging over his mantle without really seeing it. "I'm sorry, but I can't quit thinking about Norma's call. We hadn't heard a peep out of her for a while, and now she's in a flurry again. What's she been doing, planning and plotting and lying in wait?"

He shook his head dispiritedly. "I told you, she's stirred up because I'm not going to her party for Sam, and because I wouldn't take those pictures she sent with him last night. And those things are her problem, not mine. Why should we let her ruin our day? Forget about her."

"It matters if she keeps calling. It's disruptive." And it makes me want to run away, Aphra wanted to add, but she didn't.

"She won't call again. I'm sure the party's in full swing by now."

"But what if she does?"

Isaac rubbed his temple. "All right, if she starts calling and calling, I'll have her prosecuted for telephone harassment. How's that?"

"Good enough." She took a deep breath. "Okay, our novel. Where were we?"

"Carol as a third-generation Japanese-American." He readied his pencil.

"You like that, huh?"

"Yeah. It's something we can work with. If we don't like where it takes us, we can figure something else out."

"Okay then, here's another thought. How about if Carol's mother, a second-generation Japanese-American and a widow, was put in an internment camp during the war, got sick and died there, and Carol was adopted and raised by a white family?"

"Could be interesting." Isaac made notes on his pad. "And I've got another idea. How about if Carol has a little boy, say, by a Japanese-American man, and the little boy is about eight years old by the time Carol and Henry meet?"

"Then we'd need to figure out what sort of relationship produced that little boy. Was it a marriage that ended in divorce, or did the little boy's father die? Or was it not a marriage at all, but something else? And what about Henry's background? We've talked about giving him a background similar to yours, a long-term toxic marriage and a grown kid or kids, but there are other things we could do."

"One thing's for sure," Isaac said. "Henry's going to be a straight-shooting old son of a bitch. Sound like anybody you know?"

Aphra grinned at him. "You know, Bear, writing novels is the ultimate freedom. You know what I mean?"

"Yeah, I've often thought the same thing. A novelist designs entire worlds and views the things that fill those worlds from the bottom up, then from the top down. The omniscience and omnipotence of the novelist with regard to his work is God-like because by the time he finishes his book, the novelist knows all and sees all, even if he doesn't tell all." He paused then added: "Sometimes, even to himself, he doesn't tell all."

"Perhaps this entire world, all our lives and all our doings, comprise God's Great Serial Novel."

"Then we'd better hope it doesn't get rejected by His publisher," Isaac said, "or published only to be snubbed by God's heavenly host, slapped into Heaven's Bargain Basement Bin, and remaindered."

"I can see it now," Aphra said. "Step right up, ye Seraphim and Cherubim, ye Archangels and Saints of the Ages! Earthlings: The Collected Capers can be yours for the Heavenly Price of one Celestial Cent."

They shared a laugh, and when she reached over to caress the top of Isaac's hand, he took her hand in his and squeezed it. Over the next half hour, they plunged into the world of their novel to walk its labyrinthine corridors of possibilities. Aphra was relaxing. Or she thought she was.

But when Isaac's cell phone rang, Aphra's stomach gave a nasty lurch.

Isaac threw his notepad and pencil on the floor and stalked to the kitchen table and picked up the phone. Looking at the display, he snarled, "Damn it, it's her," then pressed a button to accept the call. "Norma, I will not tolerate... Oh, Sam. It's you." Then he let out a long breath. "Son, I didn't realize you'd given Hieu those pictures. Well, Hieu didn't say anything to me. He didn't have a chance. His new job starts tomorrow, and I guess he's out running errands. He left a note on the fridge saying he'll be gone until suppertime. Yeah, it's the software engineering thing. And I have no idea where he would have put those pictures. I'm not going through his stuff, either. I respect his privacy … You're welcome to pick them up later after Hieu gets home, or I'll bring them by your place sometime. But it's no reason for me to dig around in Hieu's personal belongings and then rush over to your mother's in a huff, is it?… No? I didn't think so. And if your mother is wanting those pictures back, she shouldn't have given them to you in the first place… Yeah, around supper time. Sounds good. Have fun at the party, and we'll talk soon." Isaac ended the call and dropped the phone onto the table with a clatter.

"Those pictures again," Aphra said as Isaac returned to his chair.

"Yeah." He retrieved his pad and pencil from the floor.

"How on earth did Hieu get hold of them?"

"Seems that after everybody else left, Sam and Cheryl were talking to Hieu in the parking lot. Cheryl was looking in her purse for their car keys, and to help her see what she was doing, Sam pulled out the envelope with the pictures, and then he handed it to Hieu so he could fumble around in his own pockets. Then when Cheryl found the keys in her purse, she and Sam said good bye and took off. I guess they forgot that Hieu was still holding that envelope."

Accidentally on purpose, Aphra was sure. "Oh," she said instead. "So they're partying hearty over at Norma's?"

"Sounds like it."

They sat in silence for a few minutes, then Isaac said, "That chapter we wrote does a good job of introducing the reader to some of Henry's war experiences, but we need to work out the details of his personal life. Okay, maybe he married his high school sweetheart. They wind up having a kid or two, but they don't have a lot in common as people, and as time goes by, they become more and more unhappy." His pencil flew across his pad as he talked. "Henry enlists in the Army to fight in World War II, and he learns that the world is a hell of a lot bigger than he thought it was. He returns home after the war with a new perspective but also with hatred and fear of the Japanese people because of his experiences fighting them. Their kamikaze tactics could be fearsome, after all. Then—"

"Isaac?"

He looked at Aphra over the top of his glasses. "What now?"

"Are you sure you want to be here?"

"Where else would I want to be? This is my house, isn't it?"

"But isn't there a part of you that wants to be at Sam's party? Sam's there. Your Momma's there. Your daughter-in-law and grandchild-to-be are there. Your whole family is there."

"You're wrong, Kitten. My whole family isn't there. Hieu's not there, and neither is Greg. And you're not there because you're with me, where you belong."

She liked that: with him, where she belonged. "Still, it doesn't make you feel like an exile from your tribe?"

He snorted. "No less than when I lived in that storage building for years and years."

"I'm driving you crazy, aren't I?"

"No, you're not."

"You had another nightmare last night. Where else could they be coming from, other than from the stress of integrating me into your life?"

"I've told you again and again, it's an adjustment. Things will work out, if you'll just let them."

"Tell me the truth. If I weren't around, would you go to Sam's party this afternoon?"

"Not just no, but hell no. Do you think an afternoon with Norma, in that house, is my idea of time well-spent?" He looked at her more keenly. "And you're forgetting something."

"What?"

"Norma wouldn't have invited me to Sam's party if it weren't for you being in my life. Hell, she wouldn't have had a party for him at all, I'll warrant. She sure didn't throw a party for him last year, or any year since we've been divorced. You've got to stop romanticizing what doesn't need to be romanticized. Why do you women insist on seeing hearts and flowers where there's nothing but muck and junk?"

Aphra didn't know how to answer that. But he'd made good points. She couldn't deny it.

Sam would be coming by to pick up those photographs, and Aphra had no doubt that he would, at every opportunity he could manufacture, wave the pictures under her nose, forcing her to look at them again. Ouch, ouch, ouch. She understood that the things represented by the photos happened. She'd understood it since she was a teenager and began reading Isaac's books. But photos brought the past into the present like nothing else could do.

And circumstances being what they were, there would be many more such ouchies over the long haul. She had to get hold of herself. Buck up. So she could keep her promise to Isaac and hang in there.

But how could she keep from slipping into self-imposed irrelevancy, as though it were her duty to step aside and give failed Camelot a chance to realize its potential for glory? How could Aphra keep sight of the truth: that she, and no other woman, was the Lady in Isaac's shield? An oceanic chasm lay between her intellect (what she knew to be true) and her heart (what she feared might be true.) She had to find a way to connect the shores. To build a bridge of rationality over the bottomless dread.

Writing, as she'd commented to Isaac earlier, was the ultimate freedom. Worlds to create, bonds to form, lives to mold. How delightful it would be to recreate Isaac and herself in a universe of their mutual making, a universe of pure mind made up of the Ideal Forms which reflected as spectral shadows on the walls of the cave of their everyday lives—a realm where their love, unfettered and unhindered, might be given its fullest expression. With no Norma. No First Family. A place where Isaac was and ever would be hers. All hers.

It wasn't that Aphra didn't accept Isaac wholeheartedly in the universe they inhabited. She did. She appreciated Isaac's past. Its disappointments and its adversities, used as chisels in time's unflagging hands, had carved out the man he was today, just as her past had shaped her. And she hoped Sam could come to accept her. She would welcome him as a cherished part of her life and her family, and she'd love to be a cherished part of his life and family, too.

But she was getting ahead of herself. She and Isaac touched lifetime commitment as though it were a sleeping giant they were afraid to wake because they didn't know whether the colossus would be kind or cruel.

At any rate, was it silly to find pleasure in what might have been, far outside a stone's throw from the cave of flesh and blood existence? A novelist could live many lives in one. A novelist himself, Isaac understood that. He must.

"Bear, I have an idea."

"What's that?"

"I don't want Carol to have a little boy from a prior relationship. And I don't want Henry to have any kids, either. We'll say his first wife was sterile or something."

Isaac looked at Aphra bemusedly, his pencil's eraser idling by the corner of his mustache. "Well, okay."

"I'd rather Carol and Henry have a child together."

Isaac lay his pencil on his pad and his mouth became a tight, bloodless line. "Whatever you want to do."

"Well, don't you think it's a neat idea?"

"Doesn't matter to me one way or the other."

"Okay then, here's how we could do it. How about if Carol, like me, has never been interested in having kids. And Henry is an older fellow who's never had kids and doesn't want any. But once they get to where they're making love regularly, Carol winds up pregnant. After all, birth control was less reliable in those days. So she and Henry have some major thinking to do, and after a come-to-Jesus talk, they decide to keep the baby instead of adopting it out or risking Carol's life with an illegal abortion."

"Well, you've certainly given this a lot of thought, haven't you?" Isaac asked.

"No. Actually, I haven't," she replied, startled by the scorn that had oozed from his tone. "At least not until just now, off the top of my head. But don't you think it would be a special thing for you and I, as co-authors and as lovers, to let our characters share something together that we don't and never will in our real lives?"

"I guess."

"Really?"

"Yeah."

"You don't sound very enthused."

"Well, you sound a little too enthused, if you ask me."

She goggled at him. "Say again?"

"My vasectomy isn't going to fail, you know. Those tubes have been burned, do you understand? Cut and burned."

"And I'm glad about that, too. What's your point?"

"I know what this means," Isaac declared.

"What? I thought it meant we're writing a book together."

"It means that sooner or later, you'll start whining around about wanting a baby."

"Oh, good Lord. I'm not Norma, all right? I don't want a baby any more than I ever have. I just want ..." She had to stop, having no idea how to put into words what she wanted.

"Go on. I'm listening." Isaac folded his arms across his burly chest.

"I want to know—" To know what? She backed up and started again. "I guess I want to create a perfect universe of sorts for us, where it's you and I who are bonded in the way that, in real life, you and Norma are."

"Damn it, Aphra, you throw that 'bond' and 'share' shit in my face every chance you get. And once and for all, I don't 'share' any 'bond' with Norma except for the one you're blowing up in your mind from a molehill to a mountain. What the hell's gotten into you, anyhow? Prattling pie in the sky, bliss ninny garbage about perfect universes and such. There's only one universe I know of, and it's far from perfect."

"No, no. Let me start over. I'm not expressing myself well. I shouldn't have said 'perfect.' What I'm trying to say is that the book could be a chance for us to experience our love as it might have been if—"

"Look here, I'm not stupid, and don't you treat me like I am. I don't want any more children under any circumstances, okay? Not an adoption, not a damn vasectomy reversal, by God not even immaculate frigging conception. I'd rather be dead than do all that over again. It harelips me to think about it. And me going on fifty-four years-old." He uncrossed his arms and smacked his palms on his jean-clad thighs.

"Isaac, that isn't what I'm saying. I'm not manipulating you, and I don't think you're stupid. All in the world I want is—"

He leaned toward Aphra and speared her to her chair with his gaze. "I know all too well what you're saying. Do you think I'm overlooking the significance of what we're calling this book?"

Dimly, she recognized what she'd come to think of as his Military Commander Tone.

He continued. "And I'm telling you that if a baby is the substance of what you're hoping for, there's no way I'm raising any more children other than the one I've already raised. Have I made myself clear?"

HOOAH, Aphra wanted to yell, as though she were a raw recruit replying to a drill sergeant. Instead, she replied with, "Yes, you have. Enough already."

For she needed no further discourse to grasp the essence of what he'd said: even on a purely theoretical level, the Realm of the Ideal Forms which could be theirs and theirs alone, Norma was the one woman, the sole woman, with whom Isaac would choose to share a child. Again and again. Always with her, Norma as the substance, never as the shadow. From time's beginning to time's end: Norma, and Norma's son. Never Aphra, never Aphra's child, no matter how, no matter what. In all realms, even those of Pure Mind, only Norma's genes were acceptable to be intertwined with Isaac's. Only Norma's child was worthy of his love. Norma's child was the light of his life, and Aphra's child, who would never even exist, was his fate worse than death.

And Aphra wasn't just a shadow; she was a fool. How could she have thought that after thirty years spent with Norma, he could feel differently? The deepest grooves were those which were worn by time. Sometimes, as Isaac pointed out, a novelist didn't tell all, not even to himself. And though he'd denied it again and again, Aphra had, that afternoon, caught a glimpse through the cracks of his words of the Unshakable Nexus of Family that was woven into the texture of his soul. There could be no denying that its name, forever, was Norma.

Norma.

Norma.

Isaac couldn't admit that to himself.

But his myopia didn't render the truth any less real.

Right-o. Processing revelation. Moving right along, Aphra could hang.

But before she did, she had to excuse herself to Isaac's bathroom for a good, hard cry, which she muffled with a towel. When she was done, she washed her face, blotted it with the damp towel, and flushed the toilet for good measure.

"Never mind," Aphra declared when she got back to her chair. Her face was set in an iron mask that was as strong as her resolve to never be cast in Norma's mold again, for any reason. "You've misunderstood me completely, but it doesn't matter. I've decided I don't want to go that route in the book after all. Let's stick with the original plan."

"You sure?"

"Yes, I'm sure. Whether in fact or in fiction, I need a kid like I need a hole in my head."

"Well, it's just a book," Isaac said. "Let's not let it run us crazy, all right?"

"Sounds good." She folded her arms across her chest.

A long, flat silence squatted between them before Isaac asked, "You okay? Are we okay?"

"Sure." She was lying like a rug. They most certainly weren't okay. Not anymore. But what could she say that wouldn't open up her ravaged heart to more hurt?

"Come here, Kitten." He held his arms open.

She didn't want to go. If she went, the tears would come back. But how could she not go?

She sat in Isaac's lap and buried her face in his neck, pressing so close that surely she'd leave eyelash-prints there. His fingers played through her hair, and when he coaxed her face up to his, she went along. On her trembling lips he bestowed a kiss, which deepened. Then deepened more. She loosed a shuddering breath; they'd be making love soon, on the rug in front of his hearth, his powerful thrusts between her open thighs reminding her that he could be encompassed by only one woman at a time, that it was their world, his and hers, where life bloomed—and it was his and Norma's life that was long dead.

But oh, didn't she now know that last part to be a lie? Isaac had cut her heart from her chest; he held it by its aorta oh-so-casually; it dangled like an appendage as Aphra herself did; yet she ached and moistened for him still. Maybe if her heart slipped through his fingers he could make her a new one and put it in. If the act of love brought them close enough.

If she couldn't be to Isaac what she wanted to be outside the cave, she'd have to settle for being the same thing outside as she was inside. As inside, so outside. One and the same.

She loved him enough to do that.

But it was cold out there. Their world was warm before Aphra knew Norma was its Queen in absentia.

Norma.

She shivered.

And Isaac drew back. "What's the matter?"

She blinked to hold back fresh tears. "An eyelash fell into my eye." Discombobulated, shamefaced, still aroused, she stumbled back to her chair, making a grand show of rubbing what she wanted him to think was her most troubled organ.

Light years stretched between her heart and her tongue, almost as far as the distance between their chairs: a starless, airless void. And her eyes were the wormholes Isaac didn't see.

"I don't believe you." He glowered at her, his face set in angry lines.

She couldn't remember what she had told him a few seconds ago until she became aware that she was still rubbing her eyelid, back and forth, back and forth. If they didn't get some space from each other for a while, she wouldn't be able to stop herself from reopening their ill-fated discussion. And she'd rather go deaf than hear more in the vein of what he'd been saying.

Worse yet, Sam would be picking up the pictures that evening. And she'd rather gouge her eyeballs out with a spoon than look at the damned things again.

It would be simpler and far less messy to leave before Sam got there.

"I want to go home. I'm tapped out on the book for now, and Sam will be coming over tonight to get those pictures. You two could use some father-son time, I think."

"Whatever." Isaac shifted his gaze to the mantel above his fireplace. He didn't look at her when she stood, nor did he look at her as she made her way to his door. By going home, was she breaking her promise to hang in there? She told herself that she wasn't. She'd make things worse if she stayed. And as far as the long haul, not making things worse was another form of hanging in there, wasn't it?

Surely things would be better tomorrow. That was, if she could get her head together between now and then.

Adapt. Improvise. Overcome.

"I'm just not up for Sam's shenanigans today." Especially, she added to herself, following this afternoon's inadvertent disclosure. "But we'll see each other tomorrow, won't we?"

He met her gaze, and his harsh expression softened. "Yeah,

Kitten. We'll see each other tomorrow. I have to go to Momma's tomorrow morning to do some work on her car, but we'll get together when I'm done. Probably be afternoon some time."

"Sounds good. I need to work on the Web site for the hospital anyway." Thanks be to all who were holy that tomorrow she and Isaac would awaken at their separate residences, him with his job to do and Aphra with her job to do, rendering her incapable of accompanying him to Maggie's Shrine of the Unshakable Nexus. The Shrine was the last place she wanted to go. She feared, at that point, it would reduce her to dust like a vampire trapped in a chapel.

"I'll miss you tonight," Aphra said. And she would, terribly. Since the first night they'd spent together, there were none they had spent apart.

"Me, too. I'll call you tonight, after Sam leaves." There was a flicker in his stormy blue eyes that she couldn't decipher.

"Yes, please do." She fought back more tears, and in that instant she wanted nothing more than to throw herself on the floor at his feet and beg him to wipe from her mind forever those terrible, hateful words he had spoken, the ones that had given her the glimpse into his soul that she didn't want. Sometimes ignorance truly was bliss.

She couldn't do that, however. If she did, the cracks would widen, not shrink.

And she couldn't beg. She had her dignity to consider.

Would he kiss her goodbye? Would he tell her he loved her? She loved him and wanted to tell him so, but the words were stuck in her throat like a blister. She didn't want to go back to her condo. Her home was with Isaac, wherever Isaac might be.

But she had to go. She stood a few seconds longer; when he neither made a move nor said anything more, she turned and went out.

She couldn't keep hold of the sword's grip, after all. Isaac had taken the sword from her when she'd relaxed her hold, then he'd plunged it into her chest.

And damn, but damn: the blade was much sharper than it used to be.

Heading home on Wilbur, fighting the urge each minute to return to Isaac's cabin, she experienced the second motorcycle ride of her life that was bereft of music and accompanied instead by scalding tears.

19. Plumb Tuckered Out

Though Aphra spent the evening working on the hospital's Web site, Isaac had dwelled at the cornerstone of her awareness every second. And when her phone finally rang at eleven o'clock, she was afraid to look at the caller identification for fear that he wouldn't be the caller.

But he was.

Awash in relief, she picked up the phone. "Bear?"

"Yeah." His tone was quiet, measured.

"It's good to hear your voice. I miss you."

"Do you want to come over?"

Did she ever. But she didn't want to go with him to his mother's house tomorrow morning, and she didn't want to be left at his cabin, either, in case anyone else dropped by bearing ouchies. "I guess I'd better stick around here. I'm almost finished with the hospital Web site. I hate to stop when I'm so close."

Silence from Isaac.

"It isn't that I don't want to see you," she told him. "I do. I just..."

"You just don't want to go to my mother's," he said.

"Well, I need to finish that Web site, but yes, you're right. I don't want to go to your mother's. Can you blame me?"

"No, I don't guess so."

He was leaving things unsaid, she knew he was, but she couldn't guess what. It occurred to her that they were playing a game of Who Can Keep the Stiffest Upper Lip.

And that couldn't be good.

Aphra tried the direct approach. "Did Sam pick up those pictures?"

"Yeah. He got them from Hieu, and then he and Cheryl left

pretty quickly. I wondered if they'd been arguing. Cheryl was acting funny, I mean funnier than usual. Not funny ha-ha, but funny weird. More of her hypochondria, probably."

"You could come over here, you know," Aphra said, relieved that Sam hadn't hung around to rub Isaac's nose in the pictures.

"I guess I should stick around here," he said. "I've got to be at Momma's early tomorrow morning. She's chomping at the bit for me to fix that car."

Aphra couldn't help but ask: "Did Norma show up along with Sam and Cheryl?"

"No. Sam has his issues with the divorce, yeah, but he knows not to push things too much."

Aphra didn't know what to say to that. What the hell was Isaac's definition of "too much"?

"I've got some more ideas for our novel," Isaac said. "I wrote them down, and if you like, we'll go over them tomorrow. Maybe start on another chapter. Would you like that?"

She'd be happy if that damned book were never mentioned again, but she said, "Why not?"

Silence drug itself out between them like a stone monolith pulled across grinding sand by bone-tired workers.

"There's something else I want to talk to you about," Isaac said slowly. "Not on the phone, though. Tomorrow, when we see each other."

"Oh?"

"I've been dealing with a lot of stress, and I know you have, too. Those nightmares are running me ragged, and you seem like you're anxious and unhappy a lot of the time, too. Now, I'm not much on pussyfooting around. I like to fix things, nip 'em in the bud. And there's something that I'm thinking will get rid of a world of stress for both of us, once and for all."

She swallowed hard. "Sounds ominous."

"Well, it's not. It's good. It'll be the best thing for everybody. Especially for you and me."

Her heart might stop. He sounded so grave, so cool. Best for everyone? Did he want to cut off contact with her? No, if that were the case, why would he have wanted her to come over, and why would he keep talking about their novel?

He might wish to cool their romance, though. He had fought all his life. Committing himself to her would mean that he would have to keep fighting, though in this war, his foes were Sam, Maggie, and Norma. Maybe he'd decided that Aphra wasn't worth the fight, that their love wasn't worth the fight. Maybe he was plumb tuckered out.

Oh, she didn't want to think that way. Not unless it turned out that she had to. Maybe he was going to suggest they take a vacation together.

"Well then, I'll look forward to our talk."

"I'll drop you an e-mail tomorrow, when I get back to my cabin."

Her heart was in her throat as they said goodbye. She didn't have a good feeling about this.

"How can I sleep, after that?" she asked Santiago, who was sprawled by her computer keyboard blinking at her.

If her cat knew the answer, he was keeping it to himself.

20. Terrible Unblinking Eyes

By noon, Aphra had completed the Web site for Gadsden Memorial Hospital, and she dashed off an e-mail to one of the administrators there to let him know that the site was ready for review. When she clicked Send and Receive, she pulled in an e-mail from Isaac saying his mother's car was fixed and Maggie had disappeared into her house to dress for an afternoon of shopping. Aphra wondered if Isaac's mother was going shopping with Norma.

Isaac wanted Aphra to come to his cabin around two o'clock to give him plenty of time to scour off the grease of his morning labors. She decided she'd send him a reply before she left, letting him know she was on her way.

She was glad she'd slept okay. She hadn't thought she would. Instead of staying up to enjoy the o'dark thirty hours, she'd gone to bed after speaking with Isaac on the phone. And lying alone, cold without the warmth of his arms around her, she hadn't been able to stave off the tears. She'd muffled her weeping with her pillow. But her cats had known. They heard well. They understood. And in no time, Pilar and Santiago had cuddled close, balls of loving fluff who wooed her with their sweet, inquisitive voices.

"What's wrong, Mom?" they had asked. "What's wrong?"

"It's okay," she assured them. "He'll come back."

If only she'd felt as confident as she sounded. But their purrs had lulled her to sleep.

When she fetched the mail from her box outside, it was raining. The sky was stony gray, and the raindrops were less a shower than a continuation of the dank clouds to earth, buffeted by a breeze that was chilly for late May. From the murk of her mind erupted a snippet of lyrics about the sky crying, from a song written by someone who sang the blues.

On a business-sized envelope at the bottom of a stack of junk mail, Aphra recognized her handwriting: lo and behold, it was the self-addressed, stamped envelope she had sent along with her submission to The Blotter. The envelope was thick: they had returned her story. A rejection. It had to be. And what if, upon each page, they'd rubber-stamped the words, "This sucks golf balls through garden hoses"? If that was the case, she'd run the wretched story through her shredder and expel its electronic archetype from her hard drive. She didn't need this shit today.

She perched on her loveseat and ripped open the envelope. It was indeed her story she withdrew, but instead of rubber stamped insults, she saw red scribbles in the margins. Feedback – could it be? And if she wasn't mistaken, some of the scribbles were words of praise.

The editor of The Blotter, Sandra Holland, had laughed at the same portions of Aphra's story that Isaac did. She liked the way the story explored life's patterns and parallels. And she liked Ellen, the protagonist. She wasn't fond of the story's ending, however, and opined that it could be brought around to better suit Ellen's personality. Better, Sandra suggested, to cut out the part about the little boy being a buddy of Ellen's and the part about inviting her to sing at his birthday party. Did it fit Ellen's diffident nature for her to have a little boy as a buddy or to view the prospect of a noisy children's party with anything other than dread? Sandra thought not. Wouldn't the story be cleaner, Sandra asked, truer and more poignant, if it was on the basis of having had the little boy as her sole appreciative audience, a neighbor known to her only by sight who chanced to hear her voice through an open window, that Ellen could imagine a future Karaoke night where she might allow herself to shine?

Aphra had to admit, it made sense.

Though her story had been rejected, Aphra was encouraged by the red lines Sandra Holland had penned across the bottom of the last page. It read: "Dear Miss Porter: Though I must decline your story for publication at this time, please feel free to submit to us again. Your work shows promise, and I look forward to reading more of it."

Aphra met the gaze of Santiago, under whose emerald-eyed scrutiny she'd been laboring for the past ten minutes. He sat on his furry haunches, waiting for a verdict.

"She likes it," she told him with a smile. "At least she likes parts of it, and that's a start."

Her Optimism Quotient couldn't help but rise. Maybe this writing thing could go somewhere after all. Isaac had been right, telling her to give herself a chance.

Isaac. There was no one in the world with whom she'd rather share her happiness. He would understand like no one else could. If Aphra called Di and told her, she'd be happy Aphra was happy, but her words would be spoken in the key of, "Why are you so happy about a rejection, Alf?" Di was a store manager, not an artist. And the Earth Mother wouldn't relate at all. She didn't take Aphra's writing goals seriously. She acted like she did, but she didn't. Her attitude had all the earmarks of humoring Aphra along while secretly hoping that someday Aphra would come down to earth and stop wasting her time. Mom liked to say, You're thirty-three, Alf, and really, what have you done with your writing for all those years? Not much, she'd say sagely, not much. And Bodhi, though supportive of Aphra's literary ambitions, wrote philosophy papers which were accepted without fanfare into the disinfected halls of academia. The struggles of the writer of fiction – and the gradations of rejection from soul-crushing to encouraging – were alien territory to him.

But Isaac knew. He'd been there. Not only had he been there, but he knew exactly who Aphra was.

She looked at her watch: twelve-thirty. She could make it to his cabin by one o'clock. She was too excited to wait until two. If he had yet to finish cleaning up when she arrived, perhaps he wouldn't object to her joining him in the shower.

And if he was wanting to cool their romance, then perhaps— just perhaps—she could change his mind.

It was still raining when she went out, which was a pity because she found herself gripped by a visceral craving for an open-air ride on Wilbur. But the weather couldn't oblige her whims. Her Scarab would have to do.

The Scarab carved a bug-shaped path through the drizzle to Isaac's cabin, and to keep from becoming hypnotized by the swoosh and click of the windshield wipers, Aphra considered the envelope that rested on her passenger seat. She wondered if Isaac would agree with Sandra Holland's suggestions for revisions or if he would thunderously proclaim that the woman had shit for brains and that Aphra should keep her story as is and send it elsewhere.

Regardless, he'd be thrilled that she had got positive feedback. He'd be proud, too. And though she was safely out of groupie mode, Isaac was still Aphra's hero, even more so than when he was a distant personage. She wanted to make him proud.

It was easier to focus on how he'd react to developments with her story than on what the substance of their upcoming talk would be. She'd like to pray that her fears would turn out to be groundless, but as she hadn't prayed much in her life, she didn't know where to start.

Aphra turned onto Isaac's road and glanced at her watch. Five minutes after one. She'd made good time, considering the rain. In her excitement over the communication from *The Blotter*, she'd forgotten to reply to Isaac's e-mail. She hoped he'd be pleased that she'd decided to come early.

She started into the last curve she'd traverse before Isaac's cabin came into view, geared down, and moved her foot toward the brake. And when she saw the cabin emerge from the drizzle, she also saw that, damn it, three vehicles were parked in his driveway: the Scrambler, Maggie's Escort, and ...

Norma's Neon.

She wouldn't stop at the cabin. There was no way. She had no wish to be in the company of the Unshakable Nexus, nor that of any of her minions. But there was nowhere to turn around save Isaac's driveway, so she'd have to go down the road, past his cabin, to find a suitable place. Then she'd drive back to the main highway and grab a hamburger at the fast food joint there. She'd make sure that she arrived at Isaac's cabin a few minutes after two o'clock at which time, Norma, Sam, and Maggie would—*please, please, please be gone.*

Aphra shifted her foot away from the Scarab's brake, and though she tapped the gas pedal, she didn't gear back up. Curiosity kept her speed low. And clumps of fog notwithstanding, she saw far more than she wanted to. A clutch of people was gathered on the flagstone walkway under the eaves of Isaac's cabin. Maggie was there, though Isaac had said in his e-mail that she was going shopping. Sam was there, but not Cheryl. It was probably his lunch hour; Aphra assumed Cheryl was at work.

Something had evidently waylaid Maggie from her shopping, something important enough for her to bring Sam, and Aphra was double-dog damned if that something wasn't a Lightfoot Family Reunion—or more specifically, a reunion of its parental units. Norma was in Isaac's arms and they stood between Sam and Maggie, in the center of the familial assemblage as all good nexuses should, for they were each other's nexus, were they not—hadn't Isaac let Aphra in on that very fact yesterday?

Norma clung to Isaac as the brim of his Outback hat sheltered them both, and oh God, oh God but his arms were encircling her, too, making her not only the Unshakable Nexus of his Family in all Realms Both Real and Imaginary, as she was, had been, and ever would be, but also the Unshakable Nexus of his Embrace in This Realm Both Foggy and Rainy. *Please God no, please no.*

Aphra had remembered how to pray.

But it was too late now.

This must be what Isaac had wanted to talk to her about this afternoon: he and Norma were reconciling. Driving by, Aphra absorbed additional details: Sam standing with his back to Aphra, his hand on his mother's shoulder, seeming to shiver with joy at the restoration of his family; Maggie facing Isaac and Norma from the side closest to the cabin and her face, though blocked from Aphra's sight by the happy couple, surely beaming its satisfaction. That was all Aphra could absorb before the image of the cabin and those in front of it retreated to her rear view mirror to be shrouded by a miasma of rain.

For the first time that day, Aphra was glad of the nasty weather. She didn't think any of them had seen her, involved as they were in one another. The sound of the Scarab's engine wouldn't be distinguishable, muffled by the sound of the rain and the wind, from one-hundred or so yards away. Aphra was an anonymous pair of headlights in the mist. If, after turning around, she could pass by Isaac's cabin unnoticed, she'd have a shot at the main highway, and home.

But if they noticed her at such a poignant moment, would any of them care? Look, there goes that *Abra*, Norma would say, pointing an impeccably manicured nail at the road. You'll have to root her out, Isaac, like a bad tooth. Don't you know those biker chicks are all the same? And as Isaac concurred, it might not occur to him that, yet again, Norma had mangled Aphra's name. Aphra wondered if Isaac had intended to tell Norma and Company to leave for a short while so he could have his Dear Jane talk with Aphra in private or if he would have kept Norma and Company lurking in the wings until Aphra left—listening, mocking, and finally, celebrating.

Aphra swerved hard into the next driveway she came to, a gravel trail a quarter mile away which led to a trailer on the opposite side of the road from Isaac's cabin. And tooling down the road, heading back the way she'd come, Aphra strove, as she passed Isaac's cabin, to keep her gaze away from the tableau unfolding under its eaves, but she couldn't help but spare a second glance. The same sight presented itself through the haze: Norma clinging to Isaac, Sam with his hand on Norma's shoulder, and Maggie looking on. It was as though they were ice statues that had somehow survived from winter to spring, the fog and mist what remained of snow that once was, and Aphra wondered if any one of them had moved, even to breathe, since first she'd passed them by.

It was the last glimpse she'd have of any of them. She wouldn't allow Isaac to grace her with his Dear Jane talk. The picture was clear, made more clear by what she'd seen than could be done by Isaac's words, it was more stark in its significance than any photograph. And she wouldn't accept his pity. She wouldn't give him the chance to offer it. No matter how deep her wound, no matter how critical the loss of blood, she would reclaim her sword and die with it in her hand.

Heading out of Solway back to Knoxville, she stopped at the burger joint on the Oak Ridge Highway, but not for the purpose she'd imagined. The last thing she wanted was food. What she wanted was to rid herself of the envelope that rested on the passenger seat. It had become dangerous to her. As long as it lived, Aphra couldn't. It was a symbol of what could never be.

She shredded the envelope and its contents into fine confetti and scattered it into the receptacle that sat outside the main door of the establishment. While she carried out her mission, the drizzle chilled her more than it should have, and when she returned to the driver's seat of her Scarab, she sat and shivered for what had to be five full minutes before she was able to get on the move again.

It wasn't that she was giving up writing. Writing might well be what kept her going in lieu of a warm, beating heart. But this story, *Learning to Float,* was redolent of Isaac's kind words and his hearty chuckle. *Learning to Float* was the first story of Aphra's that Isaac had read; that's why it had to be killed. There would be other stories to write, stories he'd never see, stories that wouldn't set up in the halls of her mind the painful, hollow echoes of his voice.

She couldn't remain friends with him after this. She wished she could, but it wasn't possible. The way she loved him, she wouldn't be able to bear it.

Bear. She shouldn't have said bear.

For she must kill the hope she'd tenderly nurtured: her hope of sharing forever—whatever forever anyone might enjoy within a finite human lifetime—with Isaac. That sorry little hope must be sealed away without mercy into a subterranean crypt to die of suffocation. Friendship with Isaac would siphon to her languishing hope a whiff of fresh air from time to time and would only prolong its torture. By cutting off its air altogether, Aphra would make sure that its death was quick, for she expected it to scream loudly and scream long, sucking up what little air was unwittingly afforded it upon its incarceration.

Then, please, it would trouble her no more. At least, her hope wouldn't. Her love for Isaac would live on, even without nourishment, becoming bed-ridden and skeletal yet still aware with terrible unblinking eyes, so long as any part of her remained.

A bottomless fog in her spirit condensed into tears that streamed down her cheeks. She didn't know if they would ever stop, not entirely. As outside, so within. As above, so below. And so it went.

Wasn't it Alfred Tennyson who had penned the lines: "'Tis better to have loved and lost than never to have loved at all"?

He'd been full of stinking shit.

21. Cracked

And what, when she seated herself in her office chair, did she see but the e-mail message Isaac had sent earlier to say he was back home after fixing his mother's car. It floated in the middle of her computer screen, compelling her to respond.

So that's what she did.

Composing her message to Isaac was the hardest thing she'd ever done. She told him that their lives were heading down two different roads and that forcing the two into one was looking more and more untenable. She didn't tell him what direction her road was heading, because she didn't know. She told him it was for the best that he reconcile with Norma and put his family back together and that she hoped he'd do it soon. She didn't tell him that she knew it had already happened. She told him to have his publisher contact her when his Web site required updates. She didn't tell him she hoped he ignored that instruction and contacted her directly instead.

She told him it wasn't necessary that he reply to her message.

But she didn't tell him she'd object if he did.

She sent the message, then she deleted *Learning to Float* from her hard drive and from her backup disks. Now it was really gone. Then she powered down her computer and turned off her telephone's ringer. She didn't want to talk. She didn't want to work. She didn't want to write. She didn't want to think. She wanted to sleep. Sleep was good. Sleep would make of her conscious mind a tabla rasa. Perhaps she'd wake up to find that today had been nothing more than a nightmare. But if that were true, then yesterday, when she had uncovered the centrality of Norma to Isaac's world view, would have to be a nightmare, too, which in turn rendered perverse the sum total of days she'd been infatuated with Isaac Lightfoot since she'd first begun reading his books at age fourteen. And she wasn't willing to chalk up nearly twenty years of her life to a nightmare, as tempting as the prospect might be. There had been good things, too.

She'd cried all the way home; her eyes were burning. Could there be any more tears in her? On her way to her bedroom, she spotted, on the end table in her living room, Isaac's novel *The Smallest Survivor*, the book he'd signed for her on the day that had opened up so much, for a time, between them. Should she keep the book? Should she toss it? How about the rest of his books? What should she do with them? Looking at them hurt. Would she ever be able to read them again without tearing scabs off wounds that were struggling mightily to heal?

She could kill her story, but she couldn't kill Isaac's books. Doing so would be like killing him. And as Isaac himself would say, don't give pain more than what it takes. Isaac was still her favorite author, and a faithful reader didn't dispose of her most treasured books. Maybe she'd be able to read them again someday. And if not, at least she'd have them with her—if not Isaac, then his books.

She opened *The Smallest Survivor* to the inside front cover where Isaac had penned his inscription, went into her bedroom, and tucked the book under her pillow. She wanted Isaac in bed with her. A light burning, a beacon in the dark. Pilar and Santiago joined her on the bed; they snuggled close.

"He isn't coming back," Aphra told them. "He isn't. Not ever, ever again."

Pilar answered her with a piteous meow that was less a "meow" than an "ow." Santiago would miss Isaac. But Pilar would miss him most.

The wind gusted outside her window, and she lay curled on her side, neither asleep nor awake. The layers of her cognizance were defined by Isaac's written words to her, the pillow covering them, and her head on the pillow anchored to their position. She wondered if her silenced telephone was trying to ring. She wondered if an e-mail from Isaac was being delivered to her account. She wondered if he regretted reaching out to her after their meeting at the bookstore, but how could he, seeing as how she became the catalyst who sparked his return to his central flame: that of hearth and family, a place where she didn't fit and never could. He was, she would think, grateful to her for pointing the way back home.

But how was she to return to her bland, pre-Isaac existence, knowing what an Isaac-colored life looked like? How did she consign herself back to fan mode?

She didn't know, but she had to find a way. She didn't have a choice. It was either that or wither until she died.

And though biker chicks might crash and burn, they never, ever withered.

Hours later, she got out of bed. She didn't know how long she'd been there, but it was dark outside. She left the light off in her office. No light blinked on her telephone. She didn't want to turn on her computer. Yet she wanted to more than anything.

Her latter impulse won. She pushed the power button and, through slitted eyelids, watched the machine boot up. Her hand inched over to her trackball. She wouldn't. She would. She couldn't.

She had to.

Click-click. In rolled a message from Di. She had forwarded Aphra a joke. Aphra wasn't in the mood for jokes today.

Then came a piece of spam trying to sell her life insurance.

Heh.

More e-mail arrived; its sources hardly registered. But oh yes, Isaac had replied. Aphra had known he would. His message was sandwiched between one from Gadsden Memorial and another from McGaha Realty. Its subject line was blank, as though he couldn't figure out how to encapsulate its contents with a snappy title.

She knew she should delete the message without reading it. He had reconciled with Norma; he shouldn't suck up to Aphra. He needed to shit or get off the pot. No more fooling or screwing around.

Click-click. Aphra opened the message. It said: "My dearest, most precious Aphra, I'd be lying if I told you that I haven't seen this coming for some time now, and I don't want to lie to you. To myself, perhaps, but never to you. If you need me to let you go, I'll let you go. Please know down to your marrow that I don't regret so much as a second we spent together and that I'm sorry for the hurt I caused you. If I gave you back even the tiniest fraction of the joy you gave me, then I may take heart that all was not in vain. I love you, I believe in you, and I wish you well. These things will never change. As ever, your Isaac."

Why was he saying those things instead of coming forward with the truth? Why was he confusing her, hurting her, making her miss what had never been and making her want what she couldn't have? He said he didn't want to lie to her, but his message was one big lie. He wasn't doing as Aphra wished, he was doing as he wished. It had nothing to do with her, it was all about him.

Where was this "your Isaac" coming from? He wasn't hers, he never was. And why was he calling her his Dearest, Most Precious? She was neither of those things. She wasn't his anything—never was and never would be, though she'd love to be. No, she couldn't think about that. Wouldn't. It was Norma, his Unshakable Nexus of Family, who was his Dearest and Most Precious. Not even in a novel—a fictional la-la land, for goodness sake!—could he stomach her, Aphra, in such a lofty position as the Nexus. Liar, liar, her pants full of ire. That's why he could love Aphra, yet wind up back with Norma.

Or did he ever truly love Aphra at all?

"Damn it!" she yelled at the top of her voice, making her two cats flee the room like furry lightning. "Damn it! Damn it! Damn it!" She yelled until she was hoarse, until her voice deteriorated to where it was unrecognizable even to herself, but still, she kept yelling. She couldn't stop.

Was she loud enough for her neighbors to hear? Would they call the cops?

She didn't care. Let 'em.

"Damn it!" she yelled one more time before she seized her trackball, positioned the pointer on the icon marked 'delete', and slammed her open palm down on the trackball's left button. When the message was expunged, she highlighted the folder she'd created for Isaac's messages, which contained every note he'd sent her since they had begun corresponding. Then she repositioned the pointer on 'delete' and slammed her palm down on the trackball again and again and again, not only consigning all of Isaac's messages to digital oblivion but also clicking on several other icons, confusing her easily confused operating system and ensuring that, when she paused long enough to blink and ease the frightful bulging of her eyeballs, all she could see on her monitor was the bright blue screen of death.

Her trackball was broken. Cracked in what was the first violent outburst of her life. And her palm hurt. It was bright red, as though she'd been slapping someone.

She was cracking up. She must be.

No, no. She didn't want to think about cracking up, or about cracks. Doing so reminded her of cracks in mirrors, the cracks in Isaac's words though which she had spotted the truth, the cracks in her that came from always being second. Second to Di, second to Norma and her son. There were people in her life who loved her, sure, but they didn't love her enough.

No one. Ever. Loved her enough.

She wished she hadn't deleted Isaac's e-mails. Now the only words of his she had, specifically from him to her, were those he'd written long ago in his reply to her teenage self, those he'd penned in her copy of *The Smallest Survivor*, those he'd written in the notebook he had brought her for his Web site, and those that would resound back and forth and back and forth, from her head to her heart and from her heart to her head, until she drew her final breath and the last image in her mind, his eyes as they'd looked when he'd told her he loved her, was extinguished along with her life. Loved her. Had loved her.

Had.

And her head was down on her desk and she was crying again, sobbing though her voice hurt from all the yelling she'd done, sobbing though she'd thought she was all out of tears.

22. Hair Bracelet

Someone was missing at this cookout. It was Isaac. How ironic, on Independence Day, that Aphra should curse her independence. She stared at her feet, loath to look up, as though she could pretend that Isaac was somewhere he wasn't as long as she wasn't facing the reality of his absence.

She hadn't been to a cookout at Di's since the one she and Isaac had attended together. Riding over on Wilbur, listening to his rumble, she'd thought of Isaac's voice. And she'd wondered if, somewhere, Isaac was riding his bike. That was kind of a connection, wasn't it?

She hadn't heard a word from Isaac since his last e-mail over a month ago. She imagined he, Norma, Sam, and Cheryl were preparing for the arrival, come September, of the Littlest Lightfoot. It hurt to think about it, so she tried not to. All of Isaac's books along with the notebook he'd brought for his Web site were put away in a box she kept under her bed, and folded into the pages of his first novel, *Red Sands*, was the letter he'd sent her so many years ago.

Maybe she'd take them out again someday.

She still wore the bracelet Isaac had given her. She couldn't bring herself to take it off.

Isaac's Web site was doing well. According to the hit counter, its traffic had gone up since its revamping at Aphra's hand. Hits had increased even more over the past month because Aphra, while working on other people's sites, kept Isaac's site in a separate browser window. She kept it minimized on her task bar, maximizing it only when she could no longer keep in check her desperate hunger to see his face.

She'd bought a new trackball the morning after their parting. It hadn't been abused.

Di's arm was around Aphra; Aphra hadn't heard her approach. Had she been standing, slack-jawed, like a zombie? "Alf, food's ready."

Aphra followed Di to the picnic table that Trevor, the Earth Mother, and Bodhi were around. They helped themselves to hamburgers, macaroni and cheese, and baked beans. Tony wasn't there; Di said he hadn't been to the last two cookouts, that he was spending his free time with a single mother he'd met while coaching t-ball. And come fall, Tony would begin classes at the university to earn a degree in Physical Education with a teaching concentration. Aphra was happy for him.

It's for the best, the Earth Mother had said, when Aphra told her about Isaac. You might want children someday. But I won't, Aphra had said, for the umpteenth time, Mom, I'm not you, and I don't want children, I want Isaac. Mom hadn't ventured a response, but she'd held Aphra when she cried.

I'm sorry, Alf, Di had said when Aphra told her. I'm surprised that happened. From how Isaac acted, I would have sworn he was crazy about you. I'd thought so, too, Aphra had replied.

She had thought so. For a while.

There hadn't been a peep about Isaac from either Bodhi or Trevor. Perhaps it was only women who felt comfortable consoling broken-hearted women.

Aphra sat at the table with her plate full of food. She didn't know why she'd gotten so much. Her appetite for food had been puny. Her appetite for other things, however, hadn't been so puny. When she lay in her bed, she thought about how Isaac had made love to her there. She'd ache for him and want to call him. But chances were fifty-fifty he wouldn't be the one to answer, so she had no business calling.

Had Isaac and Norma remarried? Was Hieu still at Isaac's cabin, and how was Norma dealing with that, or was Isaac living with Norma in Karns and letting Hieu stay at his cabin? Had Norma made Isaac get rid of King Leonidas? Perhaps if Isaac and Norma had remarried, Cheryl had been Norma's Maid of Honor and Sam had been Isaac's Best Man. It sure wouldn't have been that way for Isaac and Aphra, if they had married.

Aphra should be glad to be free of such troubles.

But all she could think was, half of her was missing.

"Four more months," the Earth Mother said to Di.

"Four more." Di speared a forkful of macaroni and cheese. "And it won't be a day too soon. These maternity clothes are already driving me nuts. Just hope they don't drive me to drink. That wouldn't be good for the baby."

Aphra remembered Isaac talking about how the letter he'd received from her eighteen years ago had planted the seed that inspired him to stop drinking.

"Who cares about clothes," Trevor said. "What I'm worried about is our refrigerator. It's always empty because she can't quit eating."

Aphra recalled the meals she and Isaac had cooked together, with fresh ingredients and creative seasonings, the best of which had been their laughter.

"Don't listen to him, he only wants pity," Di said. "And how could anyone pity a school teacher on summer vacation who won't even do the dishes or run the vacuum?"

Aphra thought about the many times Isaac had done the dishes and run the vacuum at her condo.

"Trevor, you're going to have to shape up before that baby arrives," the Earth Mother said. "You haven't known the meaning of work until you have a baby in the house. And Di works long hours at that store and can't do it all." Her tone was good-natured, but Aphra could tell that Mom meant business.

Aphra was sure Isaac had helped Norma when Sam was an infant, but she didn't want to go there. The last thing she wanted was to visualize Isaac, Norma, and Sam's Halcyon Mommy-Daddy-Baby Days.

"I mean well," Trevor said petulantly.

Mom shook her head. "You're going to have to mean well enough to do better." Then she focused on Aphra. "Alf, honey, when are you going to stop tripping over that long face of yours?"

"I don't know."

"What magazine is it, again, that's publishing your story?"

"It's no big deal. Just a new writer thing. Hardly a publishing credit at all."

"Still, Claire asked me about it."

"You told her I got a story accepted?" Claire and her husband,

Al, were old college friends of Aphra's parents.

"Of course I told her. Do you think I'd pass up an opportunity to brag on you?" Mom smiled a smile which Aphra couldn't help returning.

"Well, it's a little Internet magazine called Chrysalis, and it's for unpublished writers only. Claire and Al can check it out at Chrysalis Litmag dot com. My story won't be posted there until September, though."

"Is this a story we've read?" Daddy asked.

"No, it's my newest one. It's called *Groupie*. I wrote it the day after Isaac and I parted ways, then I revised the hell out of it because I couldn't seem to write anything else. I didn't think it was all that great, but on a whim I e-mailed it to Chrysalis, which I'd bookmarked months earlier. I didn't give the story another thought until Chrysalis e-mailed me yesterday saying they want to publish it. You could have knocked me over with a feather."

And though she didn't say it, Aphra's first reaction had been to cry because she couldn't share her first triumph, modest though it was, with Isaac.

"I know how you feel," Bodhi said. "When I write a paper that I think is something special, all my colleagues do is yawn. But when I fire off a feisty letter to the editor of the faculty newsletter, they can't seem to praise me enough."

"That's because your letters to the editor, unlike your academic papers, are written in plain English," the Earth Mother ribbed him.

"No," Daddy said. "It's because we philosophy professors are bored stiff. We notice each other only when someone gets his dander up. We haven't had new blood in the Philosophy Department for two decades. And that probably won't change until one of us falls over dead."

Mom shook her head indulgently. "Anyhow, Alf, I hope you know how proud I am of you. You're such a talented writer. I've always hoped you'd get the ball rolling."

Really? Aphra thought. Mom was proud of a little thing like her story? Mothers could be so sweet. And look, Mom's eyes were shining with admiration and respect. Was this something new?

Perhaps it had always been there, and Aphra had never let herself see it.

"I'm proud of you, too, Alf," Di put in. "I think you'll go somewhere with your writing if you keep at it."

"Well, thanks, all of you." Aphra was embarrassed. "I'm just glad I mustered up the courage to try." She might never have done so had it not been for Isaac.

"*Groupie* is an enigmatic title," Bodhi said. "What's the story about?"

"What do you think it's about?" Aphra replied irritably. "Like I said, I wrote it after Isaac and I split. He got back together with his wife of thirty years, and I'm back in my time-honored role as his groupie. He's snug as a bug in a rug with home, hearth, and family, and I'm alone among piles of his books." She recoiled at the harshness she heard in her tone; Daddy had meant well.

Bodhi returned a spoonful of baked beans to his plate. "If he's so snug, you'd think the poor man would look a lot healthier."

"What? What are you talking about?"

"Oh, I guess I didn't tell you—"

"Tell me ...?"

"I saw Isaac Lightfoot at the University Library on Friday."

"You saw Isaac? How could you forget to tell me?" She stopped herself. This was, after all, the Bodhisattva, whose mind was so removed from the humble earthly realm that he regularly lectured to his classes while wearing mismatched socks, sometimes even mismatched loafers. "Never mind that part. Did you talk to Isaac? What did he say? Did he ask about me? Did he tell you whether he's—"

"Easy does it, Alf," Mom broke in. "One question at a time. Give your father a chance to talk." She looked at Daddy and said, "This is news to me, too. You saw Isaac Lightfoot the day before yesterday, at the library? What was he doing there?"

Bodhi's bushy white eyebrows perched atop his round glasses, as though he was unable to fathom why he was being quizzed so. "Well, he was doing research, Barb. Why else would he be there? He's a writer, isn't he?"

"So what happened?" Aphra pressed.

"I literally bumped into him. It was on the second floor, where the old newspapers are kept on microfiche. I'd been to a departmental meeting in one of the rooms up there. Neither of us was looking where we were going. Isaac had a notebook, and I was carrying a stack of books. When we collided, I dropped everything. He almost knocked me to the floor, but he caught me before I could fall. Then he helped me pick up my books. It wasn't until he handed them to me that I realized who he was."

"What did he say?" Aphra asked.

"He said hello, and he apologized for not watching where he was going. Of course, I apologized, too. It was no more his fault than mine. I felt awkward because I know you two aren't seeing each other anymore, but he really is a very nice man."

"Yes, he is," Aphra said softly. "Did he say whether he's working on a novel?" She'd almost said "our novel" before she realized how silly that would sound.

"He mentioned that he was working on something related to Vietnam," Daddy said. "He didn't say whether it was a novel or a work of nonfiction."

So Isaac had ditched their book. Aphra didn't blame him. "What did you mean when you said he didn't look healthy?"

"Well, I know he's five years younger than me, but when I met him at the cookout, he looked maybe ten years younger. He was hale and hearty and had lots of color in his face. And he was so sturdy, like a bear."

"Yes, much like a bear." Aphra's eyes filled with tears and she blinked, trying to keep them from her cheeks.

Daddy didn't notice. "Well, he's thinner now. He's lost twenty, maybe thirty pounds, and he's pale and drawn. He has more gray in his hair and in his beard than he did when I saw him at the cookout, and he's looking every bit his age, if not older. I wonder if he's sick. Maybe that wife of his is a terrible cook."

He was trying to be funny, but Aphra wasn't amused. Listening to Daddy's description of Isaac, she felt as though her stomach had dropped onto the floor and she was standing on it.

"You've lost about ten, maybe fifteen pounds yourself, Alf," Di observed.

"Was there anyone with him?" Aphra braced herself for a description of Norma.

"Not when we bumped into each other. But after we'd gotten everything picked up and exchanged a few pleasantries, a man rushed over from around the corner of the aisle, asking Isaac if he was okay. He was a tall, scruffy fellow, around the same height as

Isaac, maybe taller, but with a narrow build. Looked to be Native American. He was wearing a black hat with a feather in it, and he had a braid down his back and a blue tattoo on his neck. Did you know him?"

Did. Not do. It was like her father was speaking of people long dead to her. "No, but it's got to be Greg, one of Isaac's old Ranger friends from Vietnam. He's half Lakota Sioux. Isaac used to talk about him."

Greg was in town? Isaac had told Aphra that Norma hadn't liked Greg, Hieu, or John. How must she be dealing with this? What could Aphra be missing here?

"Daddy, did you notice whether or not Isaac was wearing a wedding ring?"

Bodhi frowned. "Well, you know me. I don't often notice things. But you'd told me Isaac had gone back to his ex, and I was curious, so I looked. And he wasn't wearing a wedding ring. But..." He paused. "Are you sure you want to hear this?"

"Go ahead."

"He was wearing an odd bracelet. It looked like it had been made out of someone's hair. I guess his wife has brown hair, like you?"

Aphra felt his gaze but she barely saw it because the tears were blurring her vision. She wanted to tell Daddy that she'd made the bracelet for Isaac out of her hair. But that would only lead to more questions, questions for which she had no answers.

"No. She's a redhead, but she dyes her hair brassy bronze."

Again, Aphra had underestimated the Earth Mother, who lay her hand on Aphra's. "Isaac was wearing that bracelet at the cookout that day. I guess you didn't notice it, Larry, but I did. He kept rubbing it with his finger. And sure as I'm sitting here, it's made out of Alf's hair. Isn't it, Alf? Honey?"

Four sets of puzzled eyes focused on Aphra.

"Don't you think you ought to talk to him?" Mom asked. Di nodded her accord.

Aphra felt their love, she felt their concern, but she didn't know what she could say that would make sense to them or to herself. Her gaze shifted to the pile of food on her plate of which she had yet to take a bite.

Why, if he and Norma were back together, would Isaac still be wearing that bracelet?

23. Hall of Mirrors

Aphra took the scenic route home on Wilbur—to think straight. She needed all the afternoon air she could get. If Isaac was wearing the hair bracelet she'd made for him, didn't that mean that he missed her? Should she call him? But if he missed her, where did reconciliation with Norma fit in? She could make no sense of Bodhi's tidings in light of what had gone before: her discovery that Norma was Isaac's Unshakable Nexus of Family, the sight of her in his arms.

Turning into the parking lot of her condo complex, she saw, next to her Scarab, two Harley-Davidson motorcycles atop which riders sat in anticipatory postures. Her heart seemed to swell in her chest. Was Isaac there, waiting for her? Could it be...? But if that were so, then why was she seeing double?

She downshifted, blinked, then looked again. Yes, there were two bikes, but neither belonged to Isaac. Isaac rode a Sportster. Before her were a bright blue Road King—a large touring bike—and a sleek, black Night Train. The two coppery-skinned riders, their T-shirts rippling in the light breeze, watched her approach through helmets that rendered their faces indiscernible. Who were they? Was she about to be abducted by Hell's Angels?

She parked Wilbur in her garage and removed her helmet, then she glanced back at the parking lot. Both riders had got off their bikes, and as they removed their helmets, she recognized the rider of the Night Train: Hieu. His new job must be working out well for him to have bought a bike so soon.

A snippet of conversation reached Aphra's ears. "—ought to kick her ass." What? The gravelly, unfamiliar voice had come from the rider of the Road King. Aphra must have misunderstood him. Hieu didn't want to see Aphra's ass kicked.

Or did he?

When the other man turned to secure his helmet on his bike's helmet lock, Aphra saw a big, blue tattoo on his neck and a black braid down his back. He had deep creases on his face like scratches in leather. Greg. Naturally. If not Isaac, who else would be accompanying Hieu? And Greg was scowling deeply.

Hieu gave Greg's shoulder a light shake and said something Aphra couldn't make out. Then the two of them headed Aphra's way. She swallowed hard. What was going on? Had Isaac sent them?

If they had come to invite Aphra to Isaac and Norma's wedding, they could turn around and leave. She wasn't going.

Aphra exited the garage to meet them. "Hello."

Hieu studied her. "Are you well? You look thin."

"At least I won't have to diet in the foreseeable future."

"May we come in and talk to you?" Hieu asked.

"This way." She led them to the front door. Her hands shook so badly that she had trouble getting her key into the lock, but she wasn't afraid of Hieu or Greg. They were both brave and honorable men. So what was ailing her? Was she afraid of what they were going to say? As nice as it was to be in the company of men who were like brothers to Isaac, she didn't want to hear anything that would hurt her. Broken places that kept getting smashed could never heal, let alone grow stronger.

Once they were inside, Hieu and Greg sat in the loveseat and Aphra perched on the edge of her La-Z Girl. "Would either of you like something to drink? I have milk, pop, iced tea—"

"No," Hieu said. "We're fine. I'm glad we caught you. We came here earlier today, but you weren't home."

"I was at my sister's for a cookout. How did you know where I live?"

"Snake told me, back when he was spending a lot of time over here. In case I needed to find him."

Greg let out a long breath that whistled through his teeth, and he glowered at Aphra as if he'd like nothing better than to pour salt on her and eat her for supper. "Damn it, Swampy, this is fugazi, man. She hung him out to dry, didn't she? Snake would shit bricks if he knew we were here."

"Remember what I told you, please," Hieu said.

"At least she didn't come riding in with some little sissy sonofabitch sitting on the seat behind her," Greg muttered.

Hieu shot Greg a stern look, but before he had a chance to say anything, Aphra addressed Greg. "Excuse me, Greg. I know you're Greg, by the way, but what are you talking about? Who hung who out to dry?"

"So much for introductions, then." He leaned forward, his tattoo in plain view: a long, blue lightning bolt which charted a jagged course down his neck to his collarbone. His face was long and narrow like the rest of him, and his gaze, with eyes so dark that their onyx irises blended with their pupils, was direct to the point of being uncomfortable. Aphra shrunk back into her La-Z Girl.

"Look here," Greg said, seeming to notice her unease. "I don't want to be an asshole. You've got the right to live your live the way you want, like anybody else. But I want to be clear about something here: we love Snake. And you hurt him real bad. He's been even worse since he—"

But Hieu, his gaze on Aphra's bracelet, interrupted. "Aphra, I'm sure Snake told you about how we old soldiers look out for each other. That's why Red Hawk came here from South Dakota. He wanted to help me help Snake."

Greg nodded. "My construction company's busting ass on a big job in Rapid City, but they can get along without me for a few weeks. My brother's second in command – he's got a good head on his shoulders."

"But we aren't helping Snake much," Hieu said. "He's glad to have Red Hawk and me around, but he's still not eating enough, he's not sleeping enough, and his nightmares are terrible when he does sleep. And he goes to your Web site all the time and he— Well, let me just say that he has been getting worse, not better. Looking out for Snake is why we're here." He paused then added slowly: "If I thought you'd never cared for Snake, Red Hawk and I wouldn't be here."

"Is everybody going crazy? I'm trapped in a hall of mirrors. Everything I see is distorted beyond recognition." A drop of water hit Aphra's hand: a tear. She wiped her eyes roughly with her palm. "Okay, this is ridiculous. If Isaac misses me so much, then why the hell did he go back to Norma?"

Two pairs of black eyes widened and two jaws went slack. Had she befuddled two seasoned combat veterans? They spoke to her simultaneously.

"Are you crazy or just plain stupid?"

"What are you talking about?"

Things had become so surreal that Aphra thought she should look around for a discombobulated white rabbit in a three-piece suit. "Well, I saw them together in front of his cabin. Isaac didn't see me drive by. It was foggy and rainy, and I'd decided to come early. But I saw all I needed to see. Sam and Maggie were standing around, and Isaac and Norma were in each other's arms. Isaac and I had been under a lot of stress and we had an argument the day before, and when we spoke on the phone that evening, he said he had something important he wanted to talk to me about, something that would be good for everybody. I figured he was going to tell me that he wanted us to cool off and just be friends, and when I saw Isaac and Norma together, surrounded by their happy family looking on, I realized I'd been right."

"As though reconciliation with Norma is something that would reduce Snake's stress." Greg shook his head as though marveling that anyone could be so idiotic.

"Then why did he want to break up with me?" Aphra asked. "Was it doubt creeping in? Combat fatigue? What?"

"Snake wasn't planning to break up with you," Hieu said.

"He wasn't?"

"He was going to ask you to marry him. He said he didn't want to let you get away."

Her mouth dropped open, but she couldn't speak. She cupped her hands around her face and stared at Hieu as though she were the subject of Edvard Munch's painting, *The Scream*.

"Marry me?" she finally asked.

"On the evening you two argued, Snake went out to get an engagement ring for you," Hieu said. "It was right after Sam and Cheryl picked up those pictures. He was so excited. The next morning, he finished up his mother's car early and went to pick up your ring. He had to get it sized down to fit you. I remember what he said the night he picked it out: 'It's hard to find a ring to fit a kitten.'"

Aphra's hands dropped like stones to her knees.

Hieu continued: "He told me you left him because you were

tired of Sam and Maggie not wanting you around and because you couldn't deal with Norma. And he also told me that lately you'd been acting like you might prefer to be with a younger man, somebody who could give you children."

"He has it all wrong," Aphra said. "I don't want children, and I've never cared about our age difference. Yes, his family's hostility was hard for me to deal with, but I love Isaac. I would have stood anything for him, for us, as long as I'd known he wanted me to do it—"

"Oh, dear," Hieu said.

Greg scratched his tattoo.

"But he and Norma were holding each other," Aphra said. "What? Why?"

"I don't know what you saw when you passed Snake's cabin, but I can tell you that when I came home that evening, Snake was sitting at his desk with his shirt unbuttoned and his glasses off, staring into space. He had the lights off, and usually Snake likes a lot of light. When I turned on the lights, I could tell he'd been crying. I was shocked because even during the war, I never saw him cry. I asked him what was wrong, and he told me you were supposed to come over at two o'clock but that you never arrived, and that you'd sent him an e-mail saying you don't want to see him anymore.

"He also told me that a lot had happened that day. Cheryl started bleeding in the early morning hours and had to be put in the hospital. She miscarried her baby at eleven o'clock that morning. Snake had just got back from picking up your ring when Sam called. Maggie was out shopping, but Snake reached her on her cell phone, and she picked Sam up at the hospital and brought him to Snake's cabin. Snake wanted everyone to come to his cabin to talk because he was expecting you to come over soon, and he didn't want to be gone when you arrived. Sam called Norma and told her to come to the cabin so he could tell her, too, though what Norma was doing in Snake's arms, I don't have any idea. But I'm sure it wasn't because he wanted her to be there. Snake told me that everyone was at his cabin for about an hour or so before Maggie, Norma, and Sam went to the hospital to be with Cheryl. Snake said he told Sam that he and Aphra would visit later, after Norma had gone. He was going to bring you."

As though she, Aphra, were his Unshakable Nexus of Family, the form and not its shadow. Oh, if only it were so. "But Norma represents everything that's important to Isaac," Aphra said. "She's the mother of his child. Hasn't Isaac spent so many years with Norma as the center of his life that he can't imagine any other woman filling that place in him?"

Greg's expression suggested that Aphra had sprouted a second head—a green one with long, spindly antennae. "What the hell are you talking about? Norma's not the center of anything for Snake. She's a hateful, icy-assed bitch. Always has been, always will be."

"But the day we argued, Isaac pretty much told me that even though he and Norma got divorced, she'll always be the center of home and family for him because she's the mother of his child."

Hieu frowned. "There's just no way Snake would have said something like that. You must have misunderstood him. The night Snake told me he was going to ask you to marry him, he got sentimental and talked about how he wished he could turn the years back and wait for you to come along instead of marrying Norma. I don't know what more you could want. That's the best thing Snake can do or say. He doesn't have a time machine, after all.

"And I want to tell you something else. I don't know if Snake has said anything to you about this, but I've been married twice. My first wife, Pha-ly, was the great love of my life. I adored her. Her love was what kept me going, even through the war. When the war was over, Pha-ly died in childbirth along with our child, so parenthood wasn't a part of what we shared in our marriage. Instead, parenthood was a tragedy that took my love from me. My second wife was Thien-Thu, and though she gave me children, she gave me nothing else but unhappiness. I should never have married Thien. I married her because she was there and because I was lonely and missed Pha-ly. And do you know what? Though I lost Pha-ly, the memory of the love we shared is what keeps me going to this day, through all the hard times I've been having. The love she gave me is a light that will shine inside me for as long as I live, helping me to find my way in darkness. That's what family is about. It isn't what someone like Thien or Norma says it's about. And this morning, I told Red Hawk about how Pha-ly used to look at me with the same love in her eyes that I saw in yours when you looked at Snake. That's why I told Red Hawk we should go see you today."

Aphra sobbed unashamedly, and for some minutes, she couldn't speak. Fuck dignity. She wanted Isaac.

"Hey doll," Greg said after an awkward moment. "I'm sorry. I misjudged you. Swampy was right, I wasn't here and didn't see. I hope you can forgive me for being hard on you."

"Well, I'm glad you were hard on me," Aphra said, still weeping. "I deserve it for being such a fool. But please, I want to go to Isaac's cabin right now. I can't stand to sit here one more second knowing what I know. I would never have left him if I'd understood … if only I could have thought about things more clearly. Oh, I've hurt him so badly—"

Hieu's soft tenor broke in. "Excuse me, but Snake isn't at his cabin."

"Where is he?"

"That's another part of what we wanted to tell you," Greg said. "Snake is at the VA Medical Center in Johnson City, two hours from here. He was in a motorcycle accident. His mom took him to Mountain Home because he needed more care than he could get from the outpatient clinic here in Knoxville. X-rays, for one thing. Maggie drove him in her car, and I followed on my bike."

Aphra's gasp became another sob. "How badly is he hurt?"

"It could have been a hell of a lot worse," Greg said. "It happened just the other day, on Friday afternoon. Swampy was at work, and me and Snake had gone to the university library so he could do research for a new novel he's working up about the late years of 'Nam, about dissolution, rot, and I don't know what all. Night after night, I could hardly get him to shut up about it. It was like he was possessed. Anyway, Snake found some of the information he wanted but not all of it, and then he and some white-headed guy collided on the second floor.

"By the time we got out of there, Snake was pretty freaked out. I guess it was because he hadn't eaten anything all day and was running on only two hours of sleep. He was trying to be cool, but I could tell he was pretty shaky in his skin. He had no business being on a bike, but I wasn't able to talk him out of riding. So when we left the library, I stayed close and kept an eye on him. And I'm damned if he didn't slip on a patch of gravel when he was turning off the main highway onto the road that goes up to his cabin. His bike went out from under him and he went right along with it. Both Snake and the bike slid across the road and hit the guard rail there. He cracked two ribs on his left side and broke his left arm. He's also scraped and bruised up pretty bad. But the thing that's getting his goat the worst is that his prosthesis got FUBARed. Fu— Excuse me, bunged up beyond all recognition. Totally wasted, man. But really it's a blessing, because at least the VA can make him a new prosthesis. If Snake's real leg had gotten all crushed up like that, things would be a whole lot worse for him. Even his bike isn't too bad off. It's scratched and dented, but it's repairable."

"He's so ashamed," Hieu put in. "He said it's the only motorcycle accident he's had in his life, not counting minor scrapes on dirt bikes when he was a boy."

Isaac had wrecked because he'd seen Bodhi. Talking to Daddy had made his memories of Aphra scraped and raw. And now Isaac himself was scraped and raw. She must go to his side, as soon as she could.

"Are you two staying with Isaac at the VA hospital?" she asked.

"We've been with him since Friday," Greg responded. "Swampy here went up as soon as he got off work."

"And since I have to go to work tomorrow morning, I'm staying at Snake's cabin tonight," Hieu said. "But Red Hawk is going back to the hospital this afternoon."

"Is Maggie still there?"

"She stays with Snake during the day, and she got a hotel room for night time," Hieu said. "Sam and Cheryl call daily and send flowers. See, Snake is more or less okay, physically. He was lucky. He isn't suffering from concussion or internal injuries. He'll probably be discharged tomorrow."

"Well, thank goodness it wasn't any worse." Without further ado, Aphra addressed Greg. "I want to go to the VA hospital with you. When are you planning on leaving? Soon, I hope? And does Isaac know that you two are here?"

Hieu and Greg exchanged another glance.

"Snake knows we made a trip to Solway to feed his snake and to make sure that everything is okay at his cabin," Hieu began.

"But he didn't know we had in mind to go see you," Greg finished.

"But please, Aphra, ride with Red Hawk to Mountain Home to see Isaac," Hieu says. "I was hoping that would be your decision. Snake needs you. He's a sad fellow, and he needs your love."

24. Half Sick of Shadows

Aphra could see how Greg could ride all the way from South Dakota on his big touring bike. It was more than comfy, it was downright cushy. As Greg's passenger, Aphra had her own seat, a Queen Seat, which was right behind his and slightly higher. The Road King had two saddlebags, one on either side of Greg, and a fanny pack behind Aphra where she'd secured an overnight bag that held various toiletries and a change of clothes.

With the temperature holding in the lower eighties and the sky becoming slightly overcast, they'd made their way to the mountainous reaches of upper East Tennessee. Aphra felt as safe with Greg as her pilot as she had with Isaac. Her anecdotal experience compelled her to ponder the notion that in male humans, the Skilled Motorcycle Rider Gene might be linked to the Bad Ass Soldier Gene.

On the interstate highway, they passed a sign that read Mountain Home Veteran's Affairs Medical Center. Greg took the next exit and downshifted to navigate a corkscrew ramp that wended its way around to a four lane highway. Rolling, dark green mountains filled the horizon.

Johnson City was only one quarter the size of Knoxville, but the traffic was every bit as bad. Two miles down the highway took them past two strip malls, three fast-food establishments, and one university. When the highway ended at a two-lane road, Greg turned left, and another left shortly thereafter put them on the grounds of the VA Medical Center. It was a picturesque place, more so than most college campuses Aphra had seen. Multiple buildings, made of brick, crowned landscaped lawns, and the buildings were connected not only by roads that provided access but also by silvery sidewalks that were shaded by trees. Greg parked the Road

King near the largest building Aphra saw.

Heading across the parking lot, Aphra was bursting with anticipation to get to Isaac, hear his voice, touch him again. "Thanks for bringing me," she said to Greg.

"No problem, doll. More than happy to do it."

"Is Isaac in a lot of pain?"

"Well, he's been beat up a lot worse than this, as you know. He's a tough old son of a buck. The hardest part is his cracked ribs, but they're giving him Tylenol with codeine. The codeine relaxes him, too, and I'm glad because he's so damn depressed." Greg paused then added: "You know, he won't even watch TV. I turned it on for him the other night. A movie was playing, *Shimmering Seascape*, some movie about World War II. And he told me to turn the stinking thing off and leave it off."

Shimmering Seascape. No wonder.

They went inside the hospital, a modern structure built onto a much older one; the corridor they entered was its dividing line. To Aphra's right was a faded brick wall with a series of arched doors, and to her left a crisp white wall punctuated by two halls marked by signs that directed visitors to the patient wards. When they reached the first hall, Greg nudged her shoulder to turn. At Room C116, Greg nudged her shoulder again, and they stopped outside the doorway.

"Snake's in there. He lucked out and got a private room. Wait a minute while I say something to his mom. I want him to have some time alone with you."

Aphra waited, and soon Maggie came out of Isaac's room. Aphra had braced herself for hostility, but when Maggie saw Aphra, she looked something close to thankful. She greeted Aphra politely, then she went down the hall, heading for the lounge at its end.

Then Greg came out. "Now, doll, you go in there and make my brother's day. I'll come back later, okay?"

"Okay."

Stepping quietly in case Isaac was asleep, Aphra walked down a short hall with a bathroom to its right, then at last she was sharing room space with her bear. She never thought she'd be doing so again, but there she was. And indeed he was asleep, or seemed to be, lying on his back in a narrow bed with the head raised at a gentle angle. Covered by a blanket from his waist down, the outline of his form asymmetrical because of the abrupt termination of his left leg below the knee, he was clad in pale blue pajamas through which Aphra saw the outline of a Velcro rib belt. His left arm was in a sling, and he wore a cast that encased it from his shoulder down to his elbow. His silver spectacles were perched lens-side down on a rolling tray that was situated to the left of his bed. On one wrist was his watch and on the other, just as Bodhi had said, was the bracelet made from Aphra's hair.

She was taken aback at the sight of Isaac. There were mottled purple bruises on his face. He was much thinner. His jaw, still covered with beard, was sharper and more angular, and there were hollows in his cheeks. His hair was grayer all over but significantly so along his temples. Had she done that to her bear? Tears welled in her eyes.

Isaac's crutches were propped against the back of a vinyl recliner to the right of the bed. Trying to make as little noise as possible, Aphra tucked the crutches behind the bed, then she scooted the chair close enough to sit down and touch his right hand. He shifted in his sleep and let out a soft snore. Codeine, apparently, was good stuff.

When she stroked the back of his hand, he mumbled something, though he was still asleep. She hoped he wasn't gearing up for a nightmare, but as long as his horrors remained at bay, she wanted him to wake up on his own. They had plenty of time; she'd be there as long as he was. It was enough to touch him, to free her hope from the cold, dark sepulcher where she'd thought it would surely die, and let it out, up and into the world again to surround Isaac and permeate him, to warm the shadows that shrouded him.

Though he didn't know it yet.

But could he feel it? Aphra kept stroking his hand, and he mumbled again. This time, though, she understood what he said: "Stay down, don't move. I won't let 'em get you."

By the sound of it, he was back in Vietnam. But his tone was different from the harsh, grating one she'd heard him use in dreams past. Now, though his voice was firm, it was as if he were talking to someone of whom he felt protective, for whom he felt responsible. He'd loved the men on his recon team as brothers and as comrades-in-arms, but he wasn't dreaming about them. Rather, his tone was urgent, tender, the way a man might address his beloved if she were in danger.

Aphra ran her hand up Isaac's forearm, ruffling the coarse hair there but skirting the raw scrapes. And he spoke again, more insistently, though his eyes remained closed: "Keep your head down and lay chilly. This won't last long. We've got artillery support. Charlie will didi out of here in no time."

"Charlie's gone. I'm safe."

He let out a long breath then said, "No, honey, he's still laying it on. But the fighter bombers will be here soon."

"Are you fighting Charlie?"

Isaac grimaced, then his body went rigid. "Goddamn it, Aphra, I'm telling you, stay down! Keep your ass in the grass. We're in the shit, don't you understand?" Abruptly, he opened his eyes. His gaze was unfocused; perhaps he was trying to figure out if he was still dreaming. His wild gaze settled on her face. Then he took in the perimeter of the hospital room in flitting glances as though he'd never seen it before.

"I'm here. Charlie's gone, I'm with you, and we're both safe." She stroked his arm.

He stared at her, eyes wide. "I've been dreaming about you. I can't stop. Every time I close my eyes, you're there. Did you step out of my dream?"

"No, I stepped off Greg's Road King."

Tears trickled down Isaac's cheeks. "If you're going to leave me again, then go. Just go. I can't do it again. I can't lose you again."

"Oh, no. Please don't."

He grabbed her hand. "I didn't mean that. Stay. For as long as you want. Please stay."

And now Aphra was crying. She managed to say, "Sweetheart, I've been wrong. I acted on something that wasn't true, and I've hurt you so badly. I'm sorry down to my soul, my sweet Bear."

"Did you say Greg brought you? Did he tell you to come up here with him?" Isaac scowled and released her hand. "I don't want you feeling sorry for me."

"That's not why I'm here. Yes, Greg brought me. He and Hieu came to see me. But they came to see me because Hieu had faith in my love for you, despite what he thought he saw happen between us a month ago. He thought he could bring me back to you. And he did. I'm back. That is, if you want me."

"If I want you?" His voice was shaking. "God in Heaven, if I'd thought there was the slightest chance I could have changed your mind but I figured it was hopeless." He took a deep breath as if he were trying to restrain something in his guts that wanted to escape. "What made you do it, Aphra? What made you just up and leave the way you did?"

"I thought you and Norma had reconciled."

Isaac blanched and made a noise of dismay. "But why? Why in the hell would you think something like that? I exorcised that she-devil long ago, something you would have known if you'd ever half-way listened to me."

Aphra nodded. "I admit, I was deaf to the things you'd been saying to me all along. And I was blind, too, so blind that I couldn't see your love and devotion to me for what it was. On that awful day, the day I sent you that e-mail, I came to your cabin early. I'd heard back from *The Blotter*. Even though *Learning to Float* was rejected, I got some positive feedback. I was excited, and I forgot to e-mail you to let you know I was on my way. But when I got to your cabin, Norma, Sam, and your mom were all with you, and you were holding Norma in your arms. I assumed you'd gone back to Norma and that you'd been planning to break up with me that day."

"Break up? But honey, I was going to ..." Isaac couldn't finish. He only looked at her, his heart in his eyes.

"I know. Hieu told me. And if you still want to, the answer is yes."

"What? If I want to what?" Poor Isaac. For a man who just woke up, he was having to process a great deal.

"Marry me," Aphra said.

He gulped another deep breath. "Hand me my glasses, please. I can't focus." When Aphra obliged him, he put them on and studied her. "And if we get married, what's to keep you from building up crazy stuff in your head and running off again? Because I'm telling you, if I get married again, I aim to stay married."

"That's what I want, too, Bear. Life without you is no life at all."

"What about that Tony?"

"What about him? It would seem that I'm not the only one whose ears were stuffed with corks. I've told you from the beginning that I didn't care a thing about Tony and that he only liked me because I was a novelty to him. He's dating the mother of a little boy on his t-ball team, and he's forgotten me completely. He's having the time of his life."

"Well, that tells me I've been a horse's ass about a few things myself." He took her hand in his. "Honey, I want to tell you, in no uncertain terms, that Norma was in my arms that day because she was having one of her Drama Queen Moments, no more and no less. Since Hieu talked to you, I'm sure he told you about Cheryl's miscarriage. And when Sam told Norma about it, she grabbed hold of me instead of him and started blubbering about how we ought to have some sort of memorial service for the fetus and whatnot. Sam was sad, everybody was all moon-eyed, and I didn't want to do anything that would make folks more uncomfortable than they already were. So I stood there like a lump. You said it looked like I was holding Norma, but I assure you, I was barely touching her. I had my arms around her the way I'd have my arms around a porcupine.

"She wouldn't let go of me, though, and she just kept babbling, and finally, I had to get her off me because I couldn't stand it anymore. I said, 'Norma, let go of me, you've already won.' And she said, 'Won what?' I said, 'The Academy Award for Sappiest Performance of the Year.' She got in a snit then and said, 'Why can't you comfort me during our family tragedy?' and I came back at her with, 'I don't want to face a firing squad for giving aid and comfort to the enemy.' She backed off real quick, and Sam and Momma looked at me funny. Then Sam, Momma and Norma left to go to the hospital. I told Sam that you and I would visit him and Cheryl there later. Not exactly the idyllic little love-fest you'd pictured, huh?"

"Not exactly," Aphra agreed. "I'm sorry to hear about the miscarriage, though."

"Thanks, Kitten. It was sad. Especially for Sam and Cheryl. They really wanted that kid. Turned out it was a little girl. But Cheryl's okay, and that's the important thing."

"So was there a memorial service for the fetus?"

Isaac snorted. "Who knows? I haven't talked to Norma in weeks. If she arranged a service, Sam didn't say anything about it to me, so I don't think it happened."

"It's interesting that Norma stopped sniffing around once she saw I was out of your life."

"That's what I'd been trying to tell you all along, over and over again. She's a hypocrite, plain and simple. She cares about appearances, not reality. Do you understand me now?"

"Yes, I do. And something Hieu said today really helped me, too. I've realized that you and I are each other's light, each other's strength, no matter who else or what else surrounds us. That's what we must hold on to. And I believe we can do just that."

"Well, I promise I'll do a better job keeping Norma at bay and protecting you when we're around people who need to get used to us being together," Isaac said. "I've made so many mistakes with you. I truly didn't understand how hard everything was for you, with Norma's mind games, Momma's rigidity, and Sam's hostility. That's all you ever needed from me, isn't it, honey? To feel safe?"

No, that wasn't all. Aphra needed to be Isaac's Nexus. And she had to tell him that. "Sounds like you've been doing a lot of thinking, too."

"Oh, I've thought all the time," Isaac said. "I wanted so much to love you, protect you, and take care of you for the rest of our lives. That's why I told you on the phone, the night before you left, that I wanted to talk to you about something that would make things better for us. By that, I meant us getting married. I figured we might always have challenges with the people around us, but that our marriage would give us a home, a refuge, that's ours and ours alone. I thought it would give you a place to feel safe. And then, after you ran off, I couldn't stop thinking, what if I'd done this better or what if I'd done that better, what could I have done to keep my kitten from leaving me? The biggest thing I could come up with was that I hadn't made you feel safe enough."

Aphra took a deep breath then said, "Oh, but it goes a lot deeper than that. I came to believe that Norma owns the deepest part of your heart because she's the mother of your child. And that would be a big problem for me. I respect Sam's place in your life, but I don't want to share your heart with any other woman."

"And I don't want you to," Isaac said. "I'd feel the same if our positions were reversed. But why would you think that Norma is anywhere near shouting distance of my heart?"

Dare she open the subject? Though the wound still ached, the words had to be said. To leave them unsaid would be to keep a white-knuckled hold on the grip of her sword. She needed to pass the sword to Isaac and trust that he wouldn't plunge it back into her chest. Then, together, they could bury the blade in the ground.

"Well, part of it was my insecurities," Aphra said haltingly. "But my insecurities about Norma got a whole hell of a lot worse after your reaction to the idea I proposed for our book, you know, that our characters should have a child together." She had to pause to steady her voice. "It was as if you were telling me that the most awful thing you could possibly imagine is the creation of a child with me, even a fictional child by our fictional characters, while your creation of a flesh-and-blood child with Norma was and is entirely acceptable. The things you said cut me to the bone in a way that nothing else has ever done in my life, not even our separation. What you said to me implied a worse sort of separation. Your words told me that Norma is the only woman in all possible universes with whom you'd share the bond that comes of conceiving, bearing, and raising a child together, and as such, Norma commands a place in your heart where I can never go, a place I can never even see."

Isaac looked down at their joined hands. "I knew I'd upset you that day, but I didn't know what to do about it. We were talking apples and oranges, and we just couldn't make the two mesh. I guess there were three things that made me act like a jackass about your idea for the book. The first thing was my memories of the whole baby boondoggle with Norma, the way she relentlessly hammered at me, manipulated me into becoming a father. Yes, I allowed her to do it, but to say that Norma colored my views on having and raising babies would be putting it mildly. The second thing was my insecurity that you might leave me someday for a man you can have kids with. That insecurity is something I've struggled with more than you could possibly know."

He looked back up at Aphra's face. "If you knew how many times, after you left, that I thought about how I'd do anything for you if I could only have you back, crazy thoughts for an older man like me." More tears rolled down his cheeks. "And the third thing is simply that I'm a practical soldier. Sure, I'm a writer, but I don't waste energy in my day-to-day life dwelling on pie in the sky things. I deal with things the way they are. I wish it had been you and I who had a child together. We'd have the most wonderful family in the world. But it wasn't that way, and it isn't that way. And whether or not we have children has no bearing on the depth and meaning of our love for each other." He skipped a beat then said: "I'm sorry I hurt you. I had no idea I'd cut you so deeply. I'd do anything to take that hurt away."

"Well, you're helping to do that by saying the things you're saying, by cherishing that part of me, the Mother, who will never exist in my actual life but who lives in my dreams of what might have been with you and you alone, the man I love. I think about it sometimes, you know. What motherhood would be like. I guess that's only natural, you know? It's painful to think that you, of all people, would scorn me for that. Maybe it's a woman thing. A woman's heart has some oddly tender spots. The theoretical can loom larger than the actual. I can see how it would be hard for you to understand. But today, you honored the Mother in me. Where before I thought her face disgusted you, today, you pronounced it lovely. And that's the kind of thing I need to lay her gracefully to rest and let the broad stream bear her away."

Isaac squeezed Aphra's hand, and they were quiet for a time. Then he asked, "What happened with *Learning to Float*? Did you revise it or resubmit it?"

She shook her head. "I chucked it. After I saw you and Norma that day."

"Oh." He frowned.

"But a little Web 'zine for beginning writers accepted another one of my stories."

"Which story?"

"A new one. I started work on it the day after we split. I didn't think it was very good, but the editor at Chrysalis loved it. Go figure."

"I'll have to read it," Isaac said. "And I want you to resurrect *Learning to Float*. If you like, I'll help."

"That would be great. And do you still want to fool with the novel about Henry and Carol? Honestly, I'd prefer to start a new novel with different characters, in the spirit of the new beginning we're creating for our love."

"I'm with you. I haven't touched the Henry and Carol novel myself since the day you sent me that e-mail. I started work on a new book, but it's no good. It's a pity-pot mess by a sorry son of a bitch who got his heart broken, and I'm just not there anymore, you know?"

"Yes, I know. Me neither." She leaned over and kissed his temple.

She heard footsteps, and when she looked up, Greg was standing in the room, looking at them and smiling. He held a small, white envelope.

"Hey there, bud," Isaac said. "Thanks for bringing my kitten to me."

"I was happy to do it, but it's the Swamp Rat you should thank for having the idea in the first place. After I've gotten to know your girl here, I've realized yet again how wise our KCS is. He knows stuff, and not only about survival in the bush. He knows stuff about people."

"He sure does," Isaac said. "Always has, ever since I've known him."

"Well, I won't hang around. Your mom and I will check on you two tonight. I just wanted to give you this." He handed Isaac the envelope. "Swampy found what's inside and gave it to me. He said he thought you might need it."

Isaac fingered the envelope, and comprehension dawned on his face. Written on the envelope was, "With a little help from your friends."

"Thanks, Red Hawk," Isaac said. "And thanks to Swampy. I mean it, bud. From the bottom of my soul, I mean it."

When Greg went out, Isaac opened the envelope, palmed its contents, and took Aphra's hand. "My precious Kitten, will you marry me tomorrow, after they spring me from this place?"

"Yes, I'll marry you tomorrow. I'd marry you now if I could. I love you, Isaac. I love you."

"And I love you, more than my life and my breath." Onto her finger he slipped a gold band with a single diamond that was flanked by two smaller chips on each side.

Tomorrow, she'd be Isaac's wife.

She had to ask: "How do you think folks on your end of things will react?"

Isaac squeezed her hand. "Momma will be okay. She's been so worried about me that she's driving me out of my mind, and she knows how much I've missed you. And Sam will just have to get used to things. After you ran off on me, he and I had what you might call a heated discussion. He was thrilled that we'd broken up, and he was planning to bring his mother over to the cabin to try and finagle us back together. I was in a nasty mood from losing you, and I told Sam in no uncertain terms that there was no way in hell I'd ever go back to his mother, that I'd sooner hang myself by a short rope. He wasn't happy to hear that, and he was even less happy with what I went on to say. I told him that he'd helped to drive you away but that I'd never tried to drive Cheryl away. I told him I'd made my peace with his decision to marry Cheryl, that I'll always treat her with respect, and that I expect nothing less from him, as a grown man, with regard to the choices I make for my own life or, as the case may be, my own wife. I hate that I was hard on him, but maybe I made him think. If he'd give you half a chance, I know he'd like you. But regardless, he'll understand that you're in my life to stay, and he'll treat you with respect. He won't be waving any more pictures of his mother's pregnant belly under your nose, by God."

"Are things okay between you and Sam?"

"Oh, sure. He steered clear of me for a few weeks after our talk, but then, there he was wanting my, as he called it, 'expertise' on a 454 Chevy engine he was working on for Cheryl's cousin's husband, and we were buddies again."

"Well, I'm glad to hear it," Aphra said. "And one thing's for sure, my folks will be relieved. They're sick of watching me mope around. Just today, at the family cookout, Mom was encouraging me to go talk to you."

"And how are my cats? Do they miss me?"

Aphra grinned. "Pilar has been pining away for you every day, and Santiago keeps asking me where you are."

She bent over Isaac, and he captured a handful of her hair and rubbed it across his face. She caressed the bruises on his face, then she kissed them. And when their lips met, their kiss deepened until the ache to have Isaac inside her spread throughout her body to the ends of her fingers, making her tingle and tremble with the force of it.

"Oh, how I want you." His voice was rough with desire. "If only I weren't all stoved up."

"Just you wait, Isaac Lightfoot, 'til I get you home tomorrow. I'll make love to you for hours. I'll blow the top of your head off, and you won't even have to move a muscle."

No longer the shadow, she was now the substance. But she had been the substance all along, hadn't she?

Aphra and Isaac, both of them and for so long, had been half sick of shadows: hers that cloaked her like a shroud and his that haunted him like ghosts. It was only when they were together that they perceived their solidity: not what others wanted them to be, theirs and theirs alone. They were each other's mirror. They were each other's truth.

The deepest grooves weren't those which were worn by time. They were those which were worn by love. The wheels of love spun faster than those of time—its treads were deeper and its tires were wider—so that after a relatively brief period under love's wheels, all traces of time's grooves were gone from life's ground.

And all that remained was love.

• • •

Thomma Lyn Grindstaff

Thomma Lyn Grindstaff graduated with honors from East Tennessee State University with a Bachelor's Degree in English and worked at her alma mater for 13 years before becoming a full-time novelist.

A native East Tennessean, Thomma lives with her husband and four spoiled cats in the mountains of Appalachia where she loves to hike. She also has a passion for music, and is a classically trained pianist who has written approximately 50 songs and instrumental pieces.

www.ThommaLynGrindstaff.com

You might also enjoy these
Black Lyon literary love stories ...

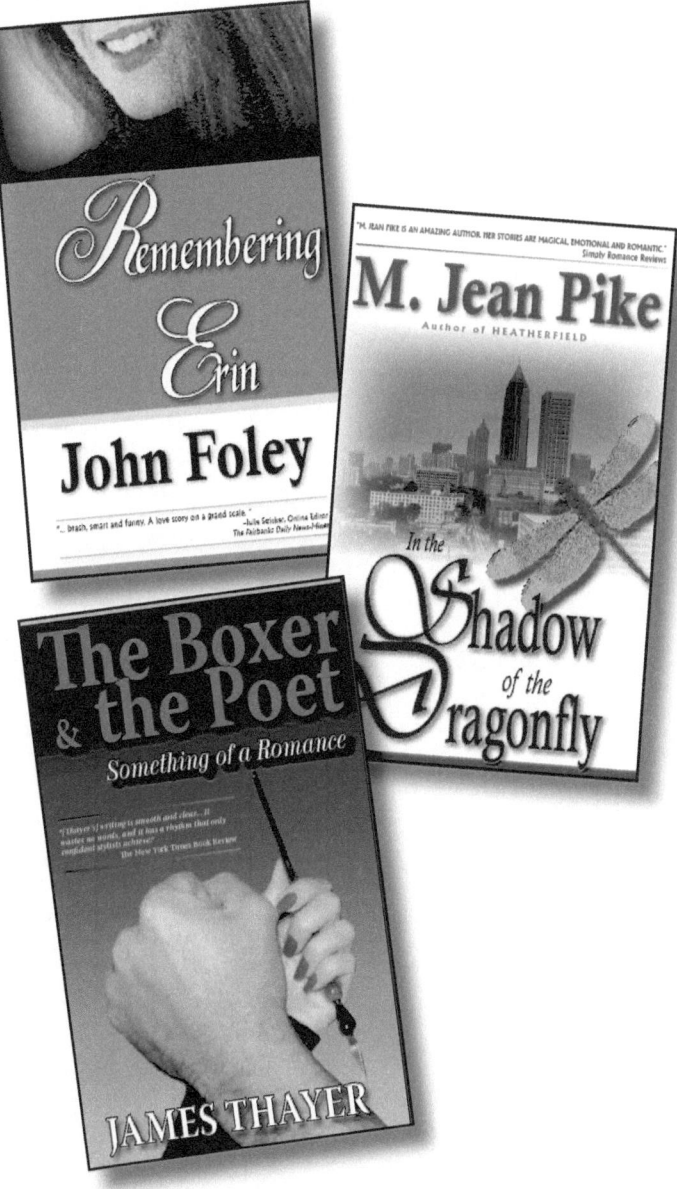

Remembering Erin

John Foley

"... brash, smart and funny. A love story on a grand scale."
—Julie Stricker, Online Editor
The Fairbanks Daily News-Miner

"M. JEAN PIKE IS AN AMAZING AUTHOR. HER STORIES ARE MAGICAL, EMOTIONAL AND ROMANTIC."
Simply Romance Reviews

M. Jean Pike
Author of HEATHERFIELD

In the *Shadow* of the *Dragonfly*

The Boxer & the Poet
Something of a Romance

"[Thayer's] writing is smooth and clean...It
wastes no words, and it has a rhythm that only
confident stylists achieve."
The New York Times Book Review

JAMES THAYER